Forty Ouncer

stories

by

Kurt Zapata

Manic D Press
San Francisco

Some of these stories appeared previously in slightly different forms in *Kick It Down* (Self-Inflicted Publications), *Back on the Swing Shift* (Self-Inflicted Publications), *Anthology 1* (Self-Inflicted Publications), and *Signs of Life: channel-surfing through '90s culture* (Manic D Press).

Front cover: illustration by Isabel Samaras / design by Marcos Sorensen
Back cover: Scott Idleman/Blink

5 4 3 2 1

Library of Congress Cataloging-in-Publication Data

Zapata, Kurt, 1964-
    Forty-ouncer : stories / by Kurt Zapata.
        p. cm.
    ISBN 0-916397-46-7 (pbk.)
    1. Rock musicians--United States--Fiction. 2. Young adults-
-Alcohol use--United States--Fiction. 3. Beer--United States-
-Fiction. 4. Punk rock music--United States--Fiction. I. Title.
PS3576.A57F6   1996
813'.54--dc20
                                                    96-35670
                                                    CIP

Distributed to the trade by Publishers Group West

CONTENTS

One Fine Summer Day

Yeah, I spent a day in the wonderful world of retail shopping. Well, actually more like a morning.

I got a job at one of those AM/PM Mini-Mart type rip-off convenience stores one summer. I saw the 'Help Wanted' sign in the window, and after filling out a barely legible xeroxed-from-a-library-book job application, the position was mine. I was now officially a convenience clerk when earlier in the day I was an unemployed nothing. Funny, I still felt like a nothing.

I went out that night to celebrate my last day of freedom because the job started the next day. Needless to say, it took many beers to drown my sorrows that evening.

I woke up the next morning in a panic. Somehow in my drunken stupor I'd forgotten to set the alarm clock. Old habits die hard. Jesus Fucking H. Christ, my first day at work and I was already late. Not a good first impression.

Grabbing some clothes, I ran out of the door. I was a couple of blocks away before I noticed my plaid shirt had a big ragged hole in one of the sleeves. It was too late to do anything about that, so I rolled that sleeve up and kept right on running. I made it to the store in record time (record time for me, that is), dry heaved once and strolled in trying to look nonchalant. Funny, I don't remember nonchalance including sweating and panting.

I found the manager in the back of the store near the dairy case. He gave me a dirty look without saying anything about my tardiness. Just directed me up front to help out the checker. I shuffled my way up an aisle. The checker introduced herself as Carmen.

She was about forty-five years old, overweight in a matronly way and outfitted in an apron that fit her like a glove. A glove that had been washed on 'Hot' and shrunken down a few sizes until it would barely fit a doll.

Well, apparently my job was to bag groceries, return unwanted items to their shelves, assist the elderly, perform price checks, and sundry other tasks that would make even the most craven boot-licking toadie cringe in embarrassment. This I did for the first half-hour without thinking twice.

The fact that I was hungover out of my mind had everything to do with it. My skull pounded with its own staccato beat, regardless of the muzak blaring right above it, while my stomach squirmed in rhythm, right along with it all. I prayed for someone to put me out of my misery but as luck would have it not a single random gunman came in that morning.

After about an hour of this living hell, Carmen announced that she was going on her break. I watched dutifully as she explained the rudiments of the O'Hare 500 cash register but nothing really stuck.

So there I was behind the counter, in charge at last, breathing pure alcohol vapors, and up comes my first customer. She was over fifty, thin, with those suspicious eyes of someone who tormented her children until they finally moved away so she had to find other targets to vent her frustrations on.

I eyed her without saying hello. She set her item down in front of me as if it was the most important thing in the world. One box of Ritz crackers. I rung it up the best I could, took her money and gave back correct change. I was pretty proud of myself. I'd pulled it off even in my pathetic, hungover state. For some reason, however, she just stood there as if she was waiting for something to happen next.

"Yeah?" I asked in bewilderment.

"Can I get a bag?" she answered in indignation.

What the fuck? I mean, the crackers were already in a plastic bag inside of a cardboard box. How much fucking packing did she need? Now, don't get me wrong. I wasn't having some kind of crunchy granola, tree-hugging guilt trip. I just didn't want to go to all the trouble to bag that motherfucker up.

"Look," I told her, "you don't need a bag."

Her eyes opened wide in disbelief. I swore I could almost see the ghost of a mean little smile cross her face.

"I want a bag," she barked out.

I looked her right in the eye and said, "You are not getting a bag."

We stood for a moment in awkward silence.

"I want to talk to the manager," she finally played her last card.

"In the back," I answered in my best bored voice.

She stormed off in a huff. I stood there wondering just what the fuck was my problem.

"What the fuck is your problem?" the manager asked angrily, snapping me out of my daze.

I looked at him but didn't dignify his question with a response.

"Did you refuse this customer a bag?" he spat out at me in complete frustration.

I wondered why he was getting so worked up, enjoying the vein throbbing in his forehead, but just answered, "Yes," instead.

"You're fired," the manager stated for my benefit as well as his valued customer's.

He turned from me and began apologizing as fast as his thin lips would allow. She stared over his shoulder at me in triumph. I took off my apron and without saying a word walked right out. Sure, I was out the hour-and-a-half pay he owed me, but it was worth it.

Childhood Hell

Something happened the other morning that plunged me back into the depths of childhood hell. I stumbled onto the bus and fell into my favorite seat in the back. I needed a place to hunker down and get my throbbing head back together after a long night of fermented self-abuse. As I settled in for the ride, I couldn't help but notice a loud crunching sound.

Frantically searching for the source of my annoyance, I spotted a small boy about four years old, sitting across from me with his mother. Immediately my bloodshot eyes focused on a canary yellow Big Grab bag of Lay's potato chips clutched in his chubby little fist. His head had to be hollow because every bite reverberated painfully in my ears. The noise from the chips seemed bigger than the kid.

They must have been going to visit some relatives because the kid was dressed in his blue corduroy best. His unruly brown hair was painstakingly combed down to one side in a massive cowlick. The li'l ankle-biter did not look comfortable. He kept squirming in his seat and humming some unrecognizable tune in between bites. His squat little legs dangled three or four inches off the ground and kicked partially in time to the tune he hummed. His mother was constantly shushing him. She did this without enthusiasm as though it were automatic. No wonder he wasn't listening to her. As I examined the little rug rat I couldn't help but laugh in sympathy. Suddenly it all came flooding back to me: the hell of being a kid.

Curiosity seems to be the most important aspect of childhood. Who can resist the image of a young child exploring the boundaries of his or her environment? For me, my curiosity took the form of science experiments. Being unfamiliar with electricity, I thought I would investigate the potential of my newly discovered power source. I stuck a screwdriver into the wall socket. Surprise - fireworks!

Ever take apart a TV, just to see how it works?

Here is one question I'm still working on: if you mix together melted army men, varnish, paint thinner, Comet, charcoal starter fluid, and anything else flammable you can find in the basement, will it make napalm? I wonder what the essential ingredient I left out was? Probably something obvious like styrofoam cups or ant stakes.

Kids never seem to run out of questions and "Why?" is number one with a bullet. However, you can never be sure if something you honestly want to know will offend someone.

I was perplexed one year at Thanksgiving, so to kill my curiosity I asked my uncle, "Why are you so fat?" I mean, I really wanted to know how he got that big. I still haven't lived that one down and that uncle is dead.

I was a picky eater. I didn't like any of the foods on my plate to touch each other. I had a rudimentary understanding of chemical reactions and was sure that brussel sprouts would serve as a catalyst for the conversion of something in leftover tunafish casserole into some powerful neurotoxin. I mean, just think of what that shit smells like.

I would sit there, pick at my dinner and go over the possibilities of having a new disease named after me because I ate some strange, incompatible, white trash combination of flora and fauna, until I had a plate full of cold piles of indistinguishable foodstuffs. With visions of fatal gastrointestinal bloating, cramping and hemorrhaging, I would do anything to keep me from going down in the journals of medical infamy.

Plan A: Push the food around the plate (movement is key here) so it will appear you scarfed, and compliment the Old Lady's culinary skill. This rarely worked, so there I would "Sit until you are finished."

Plan B: The "Look, I finished" stuffed napkin ploy. The real question here is, what to do with the napkin? May I suggest a quick trip to the bathroom for easy disposal. My mother became wise to this soon enough but it still works on well meaning yet unskilled chefs of the female persuasion. Last resort is to dump everything into the milk glass when no one is looking, but this can make for one disgusting last sip if busted.

I'll tell you what, I could never understand parents. Before my father would go to work in the morning he would generally leave me with something to do.

"Goddammit, for the last time, don't climb on the roof!" he would yell, and sure enough it was my duty to get up on that roof. Kinda like a double-dog dare. I never would know quite what to do once we got up there so usually my brother and I would horse around, throw a few handfuls of gravel at my sisters and threaten to push each other off, until the Old Man came home. He would see us, have a fit, and my day would be complete. Why do they tell you not to do something like that? To this day, when he barks out orders at me, it goes in one ear and...

Another thing I realized is, a kid who eats Abba Zabba candy bars will do just about anything. That's the kind who can flip his eyelids inside out or will eat ants. Easily persuaded, these kids are fun to hang out with but things tend to get out of hand. I convinced my friend Dave once he couldn't hit the goofy kid from down the block in the head with a rock from fifty yards in a high wind. I was wrong. I think that kid's mom still hates us.

Just like everything, childhood has its bad side also. Either you're too big to be carried or too little to be taken seriously. If I ever hear someone use that patronizing tone on me again, I swear I'll gouge their fucking eyes out with a plastic fork.

But my personal fave was hand-me-downs. There were four kids in my family, so I'm well acquainted with them. The worst was that I was second in line so I got most of my hand-me-downs from my older sibling, Katy. Nothing better for a kid's self-esteem than wearing your sister's old clothing.

And as if that wasn't enough, my parents were firm believers in Truth in Advertising. If Sears' Toughskins were advertised as 'nearly indestructible' then goddammit they were nearly indestructible, regardless of the fact that I would come home in a blown-out pair all the time. Now, practically everyone I knew wore Levi's 501s except me, so you could tell when I was up for kickball by the sound effect. I'd kick the ball, then be off around the bases, "Vip-voop, vip-voop, vip-voop," like some godforsaken human washboard. I hated those pants.

So I sat there on the bus wondering what happened. I looked the little monster in the eye and wished I had some good advice for him. I mean, something like: Never steal anything from a liquor store, unless you're absolutely sure you can get away with it, or, If you can't fix it with duct tape, that shit is broke. Nothing came to mind however, so I smiled to myself and realized he'll just have to make those mistakes for himself.

Beer

Beer. Four simple ingredients - water, malt, hops and yeast - make me happy. Yeast breaks the starchy malt down into carbon dioxide and ethyl alcohol. The hops flavor the mix. And water lubricates the whole process.

Simple yet satisfying, I drink it every day. Beer makes me feel good and gives me respite after a long shift at work. Sometimes I can't be sure which is more satisfying, the first beer of the day or the last. To gain a working understanding of the dynamics of beer, I tend to break it down into four categories.

Everyone (everyone I know, that is) has a beer they drink on a regular basis, a favorite flavor, their patron beer. A beer that you drink every night for a month straight then get pissed if a friend brings over a twelve-pack of something else.

For some it's Budweiser, others Stroh's or Miller, but for me it's... Well, let me put it to you this way: I could take a bath in the shit. I mean, a gimmick is a gimmick so you tell me the difference between the Champagne of Beers, Cold Filtered, Fire Brewed, 33, or the King of Beers. There is a veritable plethora of domestics that could qualify as a patron beer, it depends on personal taste, and mine is in my mouth.

Hell, when I was in high school, ours was a pale lager named Regal Select ('Recognized As One Of America's Two Great Beers') not widely known outside of Oakland, where I suspect it was brewed, but highly respected amongst the $1.69 six-pack crowd. Many are the pleasant memories of nights spent around a trashcan fire at John Hinkle Park, emptying a few of those cold white cans, telling lies, and waiting for the cops to come. All in that order. Yet I digress with stories of the glory days.

Anyway, another category I find myself lumping beer into is the Quantity category. This is the kind of beer you buy when sent to the store with $13.43 by eight people, $3.43 of it in change. To be frank, this is cheap beer brewed by the acre in decaying midwestern towns. This kind of beer should be consumed the same way it's produced: in volume. This style of beer is only sold in twelve-packs which is probably a good thing: nothing succeeds like excess. My personal favorite is Milwaukee's Best.

Some people ask, "How can you drink that shit?"

To which I reply, "This is America, where there are truth in advertising laws. If it says 'Milwaukee's Best', it must be Milwaukee's best."

Of course, you can't ignore the Brown Derby/Lucky Lager duo. Essentially the same beer, both brewed by the General Brewing Company but sold under different labels by competing supermarket chains, these suckers can make a party. The puzzles on the caps are usually easy until your sixteenth or seventeenth one. The only drawback: each bottle only contains eleven fluid ounces. Never drink warm, I'm warning you.

Quality is a different end of the beer spectrum altogether. This is the kind of beer I drink when the occasion demands it (usually when someone else is picking up the tab). The kind of beer you order when you just can't compromise your pride, or taste buds for that matter, by ordering wine while out on a date. Nothing perpetrates the fraud of class better than confidently ordering a Cuzco with Peruvian food or a Singha with Thai. However, don't get suckered into drinking overrated, expensive American beer.

As Dennis Hopper said in *Blue Velvet*, "Heineken? Heineken?! Fuck that shit. Pabst Blue Ribbon!" I mean, they're practically the same thing.

Last but not least are the beers meant for some serious drinking. The shit you drink to get drunk. No fucking around, I'm talking mean, belligerent drunk. The kind of drunk where you wake up the next day, fully clothed, on the floor, head three sizes too big, and pick glass out of your cuts because you broke every mirror in the house last night. They reminded you of her.

I usually try to drink this kind of beer alone because that's when you get your best drinking done, but it doesn't hurt to share one with a friend. Nothing better to bond over than a couple of 40s of high-powered malt liquor. Mickey's, Schlitz Bull, Olde English 800, King Cobra, St. Ides - any of these will do.

Ecstasy may be the Love Drug, but malt liquor is definitely the Hate Drug. This shit will make you feel like a cement-boned Cro-Magnon man right before two small Filipino boys kick the crap out of you. Drink enough and you'll fight your best friend, girlfriend, or even inanimate objects over the smallest slight, imaginary or otherwise. Ever seen someone fight a couch because it tripped him? I wrestled a Christmas tree once. Malt liquor is good for drowning your sorrows but better for adding fuel to your fire. Also perfect for extended crying jags and bouts of groveling self-pity.

Those are the dynamics of beer for me, my own arbitrary classifications. These categories tend to blend from one to another and change with personal taste. I don't expect you to cram your opinions into my narrow generalizations. It's your world, I'm just passing through.

Murio's Trophy Room

She came down and met him at Murio's Trophy Room on Haight Street It was about 9:15 on a Thursday night and she was running a little late, having promised to show up around 9. Even though summer was only a couple of weeks away, she was still freezing. The temp had dropped with the sun like it always did this time of year. The fog that had loomed out in the Avenues all day had finally crept inland. The damp chill cut right through her jacket. She didn't get it, not being from S.F., layers of clothing was what it was all about.

Murio's was fairly crowded, she noticed, after being carefully scrutinized by the doorman. A wall of regulars was sitting at the bar, not a stool open. She observed their backs. Bored, hardcore types just drinking to get fucked up. The bartender paced behind the bar, ignoring orders. It smelled like a combination of cigarettes and stale beer, with a subtle undercurrent of urine coming out of the open men's room door.

A group of five guys sat at the near end of the bar, laughing at some private joke. They were long hair musician types and each was uniformed in a leather jacket adorned with the name and/or logo of their respective bands. A couple sat drinking what looked like gin and tonics, lime wedges floating in tall glasses, at one of the tables. Aerosmith was blaring out of the jukebox, amplified just to the point of distortion, so the music sounded thin and tinny.

He stood in the back near the popcorn machine, playing pinball. Black Levi's, blue cotton workshirt, jean jacket. His short brown hair was pushed back from a high forehead, more like a fivehead, he thought. She ordered a bourbon and soda after finally catching the bartender's eye.

"$2.25," he quoted.

She laid three one dollar bills on the bar. The bartender turned back with her change but she had already walked away.

She came up to him, chuckling to herself. He looked funny. He was shaking the pinball machine violently, eyes fixed on the glass, concentrating. Arms tensed, jaw clamped shut, the muscles flexing as he ground his teeth. She stood there shaking her head, a little smile on her face, watching him. It took a second but he caught the motion out of the corner of his eye.

"Hey, there you are," he smiled, almost losing the ball he was playing. And then, "The tilt is broken. I'm close to popping this thing," as if to explain himself.

His ball was still in play. She looked up at the chalkboard behind his head. His initials were about seven names down on the list for the pool table, with three more trailing behind. She turned to watch the two guys playing on the table. They were down to the last two skittles and the eight ball. The more sober of the two was winning. A couple of hippies and their girl watched from the rail. Probably next player up, she decided.

He quickly lost the ball he was playing to one of the side alleys and the next, his fifth and final ball, freight trained right down the middle because he kept stealing glances over at her. It made him lose his rhythm, shaking the machine too late to save his ball. He turned around in disgust without waiting to see if he matched for a free game, which he didn't. Led Zeppelin was now playing on the jukebox, he noticed, making his defeat seem that much more sour.

He hated The Mighty Zep, never really getting their appeal.

They stood watching the reigning champion of the pool table sink the eight ball. One of the spectators detached himself from the rail, knelt, and fed two quarters into the machine. The winner stood chalking his cue with a confident smirk on his face.

I hope that guy loses, he couldn't help but think to himself.

He picked the Rolling Rock up off the table next to the pinball machine and drained the remainder. She was almost done with her bourbon and soda.

"You wanna go down to Deluxe?" he wondered aloud.

She nodded her head in agreement and sucked up the rest of her drink through the little stirrer/straw thing. They pushed their way through the bar, out of the doors, and onto Haight Street. She hesitated briefly until he caught up.

"It's cold," she stated, pulling the jacket tighter around her.

"Yeah," he agreed dumbly.

They started up the block toward Deluxe. He wanted to tell her about something that had happened at work but the whole thing sounded like sour grapes on his part. Whining wasn't a pretty thing.

"You're lucky to have a job," the voice of his father echoed in his head. Worst-case scenario, the streets weren't a far fall. A couple of bad breaks and the curb could have been his pillow. He looked up at one of the telephone poles as they passed. It suddenly hit him and he had to laugh.

"I just realized what I want to do with my life," he began.

She looked at him, puzzled, but he went on nevertheless.

"Have you seen those 'Jobs for the Environment' flyers printed on unrecycled and unrecyclable yellow overdyed cardstock? That's what I want to do. Go from neighborhood to neighborhood littering the streets in the name of the environment and get paid for it. You know, under every windshield wiper, a stack on each front porch. Man, the irony of that..."

He realized that he had trailed off mid-sentence and stood mutely in the sidewalk. He stared at a figure lying in a doorway up the block.

"Hold on a second," he explained, ducking through the open door to Escape From New York Pizza. "I wanna get a slice."

Confused, she watched him take his place in line behind the only other customer. He didn't usually like to eat when he was drinking. From the doorway where she was waiting, she heard him ask for a slice of cheese. The girl with her lip pierced took his order and the one with her nose pierced took his money. It made perfect sense to him in a way.

He turned and walked out without bothering to shake any spices on the slice. She noticed he made no actual motion to eat it. They started back up Haight Street, the wind blowing against their backs. Now it really was cold.

They had walked for a few yards when she was about to ask about the slice. Before she could, he stopped at a doorway and crouched down on his haunches. An ancient looking vagrant was sitting just inside.

"Hey, Old Man," he told him, "I ain't hungry. Eat this slice."

The old bum took the paper plate and smiled through his drunken haze.

"Thanks, man," the words slurred over cracked and peeling lips.

He heard the old guy cough and an empty bottle tip over next to him. It made him feel sad, but when the choking stopped he looked back and saw the old man biting into the slice. She didn't know what the fuck to make of it and walked along staring at him. What made him do that? she wondered.

He stared down at his falling feet, shoulders hunched against the cold, a look she didn't recognize on his face. He saw her staring out of the corner of his eye. It didn't bother him, he just wondered how to explain himself. It took a couple of seconds but the pieces fell together soon enough.

"One night I was drunk," he began. "I was walking home from Murio's and this derelict spare changes me for beer, straight up. Only he was asking my knees because someone had just rolled him and he couldn't stand up. I mean he was all fucked up: one eye swollen shut, blood on his face. I was gonna step over him but I just couldn't bring myself to do it. This was a human being. I knelt down and asked him what happened.

"I guess he thought I meant 'What happened to bring you to a doorway on Haight Street?' not 'What happened to your face?' because I got a ten minute horizontal stream-of-consciousness performance.

" 'My daddy told me two things. Two rules. Number one? Number one was never fight with the woman. You can't win. That's rule number one: Never fight with the woman. She is always right. That is what my daddy told me. The woman is always right. She is unable to see past her faults. You can't win. Never fight with the woman. She is always right. That's rule number one. Never fight with the woman. You can't win.

" 'Now rule number two. What was rule number two? My father told me two things. One was never fight with the woman but what was the other one? I should remember it. Number two of the two things my daddy told me. What was it?...' with that the bum trailed off, shutting his eyes. For a second I thought he was dead. It scared the shit out of me. I was about to call for a cop but the old guy smiled and murmured something about 'never fight with the woman'.

"I realized he was asleep. I didn't know what to do so I left him in the doorway to sleep it off."

He stopped because they had reached the front door of Deluxe but also because he wanted to finish the story.

"That old guy will be dead soon. Just some worthless old derelict found face down on Haight Street but there had to be more to him than that."

Pulling open the door, they stepped into the smoke and attitudes.

The Hate Man

We called him the Hate Man. Scrawny little guy with a red matted beard that leapt out from his jaw in all directions. Typical Salvation Army street vagrant clothes, encrusted with the residue of countless dumpster dives, followed by nights of sleeping in Telegraph Avenue's urine-soaked doorways. He had those piercing eyes usually reserved for the criminally insane, religious zealots, seagulls, and sewer rats. The kind that bored into yours at a glance like hard points of glass.

There was a reason we called him the Hate Man. His mission in life seemed to consist of standing on one of Telegraph Ave's many corners and ridiculing people as they passed by. I mean, he could hurl abuse at sorority girls, businessmen, punkers: no one was immune to his sarcastic-as-a-motherfucker tongue. The Hate Man was a lean mean heckling machine.

And he always began his tirades with "I hate..."

The best part of the whole affair was the fact that everything he had to say was 100% Grade AA fucking true. The Hate Man could sum up your whole pathetic life in one simple throwaway sentence, leaving you feeling about one inch tall. I should know because it happened to me the first time I laid eyes on him.

I passed by what I thought was just another harmless street crazy, when the Hate Man said something so cutting and precise I stopped dead in my tracks. When I turned to ask why he wanted to maddog me for, I was confronted by someone who had absolutely nothing to lose. There wasn't anything I could do to him that hadn't been done before and he knew it. The Hate Man was in charge of the situation the whole way. Before I could decide on a reply, he had already moved on to jeer at two or three others. I liked the Hate Man's honesty and determination - he would fuck with anyone - so I used to go up to Telegraph just to check him out.

Many were the times I was privileged enough to witness the Hate Man's antics. It was great. He could halt a passerby with one sentence and trade insults with the best of them.

One day - I wasn't there, but I got to hear all the gory details later on - the Hate Man assembled a crowd on the steps of UC Berkeley's Sproul Hall, and with the assertion of his actually being Jesus Christ, reached up and pulled his eyeballs out of their sockets. Jesus Christ was right!

So I hadn't seen the Hate Man in a while. Telegraph Ave seemed a little emptier and quieter than usual, but that old proverbial vacant street corner was always quickly filled by another unique graduate of our progressive mental health system, so I soon forgot about him.

Well, one fine spring day me and my friend Jim were strolling down Telegraph after having just slammed a 40-ouncer of Mickey's Malt Liquor apiece in the public parking lot on Durant. We were discussing the merits of jacking off with one's left hand as opposed to the usual right (feels like someone else is doing it to you), when I looked to my right and lo and behold who should it be but... the Hate Man.

Only now he was sitting at a card table set up on the corner of Channing Way and Telegraph. A small folded card on the table read 'Tarot'. The Hate Man sat serenely, clutching his white cane, waiting. It seemed so unlike the Hate Man to just be sitting there that I stopped to get a good look.

"Dare you to get your fortune read," laughed Jim.

I don't take a dare well, I thought as I sat down in the empty chair across from the Hate Man.

The Hate Man didn't say anything, just leaned back in his chair as if he were sizing me up. It wasn't an action I normally associated with the blind.

"Do you want a short reading?" he finally asked.

"Uh, yeah... Sure," I stammered.

The Hate Man began shuffling the deck. Tarot cards leapt from one hand to the other faster than my buzzed eye could register. I began wondering how he was going to tell my fortune, let alone arrange the cards face up.

"Don't think I can read 'em?" he asked, catching me staring I didn't know the fuck how.

"I don't know," I answered honestly.

I continued to stare at his craggy, weather-beaten, pockmarked, fucked up face thinking about what it must be like to pull the eyeballs out of your own skull. The glass eyeballs they gave him sure looked real. Whoever 'they' are.

I would've had a pretty hard time telling those eyes from the real thing if I wasn't privy to a little insider information. They had white corneas, light blue irises, and the requisite black pinhole pupils just like the real thing should have, but something just wasn't right. Maybe it was because one eye stared straight ahead while the other had begun to wander towards the lower left hand corner of its socket, giving him an odd fish-eye look. Wonder what made him do it?

"To get something, you have to be willing to give something up," the Hate Man answered my unvoiced question as if he were reading my mind.

His cryptic answer shocked me. I didn't know what the fuck to say to it. I sat dumbly searching for words.

"Let me clarify myself," he began. "Tell me, you have a job, right?"

"Uh-huh," I mumbled, trying to follow his reasoning.

"What did you have to give up for it?"

Nothing, I almost answered, hesitating. I thought about it, remembering the interview. It all came back to me: swallowing my pride, misrepresenting myself as a conscientious and dedicated worker, sitting up straight and paying attention, the whole nine yards. I guessed that my self-respect and free time were bought pretty cheap. Just a paycheck on the 1st and 15th. It hit me like a 16-ounce claw-end hammer.

"Everything has its price," the Hate Man summed it up the best he could.

I knew it was a cliché but that statement was so fucking true it almost killed me. I wallowed in it, trying it on for size.

The Hate Man began telling my fortune, selecting three cards off the top of the deck, but I was lost. Lost thinking about the price he had paid. The Hate Man had given up his sight. Something so basic, it seemed almost impossible to live without.

But what had he gotten in return? That was the question that stuck in my head. It repeated itself over and over. I was still thinking about it when the Hate Man announced he was done. I looked up in surprise.

I vaguely remembered the reading, but I'll never forget what he said. It stuck with me like a bad feeling of deja vu. I stood thanking him sincerely, laid a five dollar bill on the card table before the Hate Man, and left without looking back.

Now every time I pass my reflection in a mirror or window I can't help but stare into my own eyes wondering about the Hate Man. I don't think I'm ready to find out yet.

The Supe

He started the job. It didn't matter what he did or where he did it, let's just say he was bringing home the bacon. His coworkers seemed nice enough but kind of dead inside. They walked around in a daze, as if the job was too much for them, never quite standing up straight. Their hunched shoulders and downcast eyes bugged him. He wanted to ask why they never raised their voices but the answer was obvious.

The first week was okay, he could make small talk. The faces were still fresh even if the opinions weren't. It was as if he never belonged, even though they hired him over three others. Couldn't they see right through him?

Monday morning of the second week was the worst. He had been up all Sunday night, drinking. Alone. Seemed natural enough to him. Couldn't think of anyone to drink with. He sat there all night, staring out of his window. Not much moved. The silence allowed him to think. Think about his life. The hole welcomed him.

He was still in it Monday morning. And then the Stepford Workers greeted him back to the job. He eyed them suspiciously, not saying anything.

He spent the day in silence. His coworkers tried to spark up a conversation but he just stared at them blankly. It comforted him but made the others nervous. They stopped talking to him and started talking about him. In loud voices, all around him, as if he weren't there. He felt like he wasn't.

Come Tuesday morning, he really wasn't. He lay in bed watching the alarm clock. He had been watching it steadily since 1:38 a.m. the night before. It was now 9:46 a.m. He was officially fifty-one minutes late. He felt free. Because he knew he didn't have a job anymore. No longer had far to fall.

He yanked himself out of bed. His dirty pants lay on the floor where he had left them the night before. They felt cold and clammy as he pulled them on again. He figured he might as well wear the socks, too. About the cleanest pair he would find, anyway. The rest of the outfit fell together easy enough. Just grabbed what was lying closest without regard for fashion.

He got off a streetcar and walked the few blocks to his old job. He felt good, actually taking his time for once. The pigeons didn't bother to get out of his way. It was almost as if they knew. The buildings loomed over him. Not threatening, but reassuring.

The door handle felt strangely familiar. He pulled the door open. Heads turned and then, recognizing a dead man walking, turned again. No one wanted to be associated with him. He couldn't blame them. The supervisor's door was right where he had left it. It was pushed open easier than he had imagined.

"You're late," the Supe stated, looking up.

"I quit," he confessed.

"Look, you can't do that," the Supe explained, "when I hired you..."

"I quit," he interrupted more forcefully, the words strained between grinding teeth.

The Supe looked down, defeated. Just stared at the papers on his desk. He had beaten the Supe but it had been too easy. He had nothing else to lose. Confrontation was what he wanted. He stared hard at the Supe wondering why he had given this idiot any power over his life. He realized it was over and it made him feel good.

"I'll be back Monday for my check," he promised. He walked out feeling better and worse than he ever had before.

My Old Man

Man, I couldn't fucking believe it. When all was said and done, I was actually almost excited about voting that year. Don't get me wrong, I'm about as politically apathetic as the rest of my generation, but something just got under my skin this time. No, it wasn't that "It's a crucial swing year" or the "Rock the Vote" bandwagon that I was jumping on. I wasn't voting because it was suddenly the hip thing to do. Fuck no, I've been 'making my voice heard' steadily ever since I turned eighteen years old.

It all started with my Pops, which was where I used to think a lot of my problems did, but that's another story. I turned sixteen about a month before Reagan was voted into office. The Old Man was all for it. Weeks before the big election, him and Moms would have long arguments over who they should vote for, which usually escalated to shouts and ended with one of the Old Man's patented shots to the head.

My father was quick with the back of his hand, thunking you across the forehead like an overripe melon. It didn't hurt so much as paralyze you with fear and anger and especially hatred.

Now Moms was a lifelong Democrat, as opposed to the Old

Man, who was more of a sporadic Republican, meaning if he did get around to voting it was usually with the GOP. I remember, even after all their arguments, my mother was still supporting Jimmy Carter. She just wasn't falling for that 'Save the Hostages' crap. Not quite as vocally as before, since she didn't want to get beat down in front of us again.

Well, soon enough those first couple of days in November rolled around. The coming election was the topic of choice to be studied in the hallowed halls of Albany, California's fine institutes of learning, so it was on all our minds.

Sure enough, we were at the dinner table one night and my sister Karen asks, "Who are you gonna vote for?" not knowing the can of worms she had opened.

I gave her the old I'm-gonna-kick-your-ass-after-dinner look just to drive home the point that she had fucked up. I could feel the tension at the table jump a notch. Moms opened her mouth to speak.

"Shut up and tell 'em you're gonna vote for Reagan" the Old Man answered for her.

I guessed that Pops figured he could just order my mother to see things his way since screams, threats, accusations, and finally the dreaded shot to the skull, didn't seem to work. Moms just gave us her long suffering look. I sat there hating myself and everyone around me, especially the Old Man. I promised myself right then and there that he would get his. It took me almost two years to figure out how.

Well, I didn't really figure it out, it just kind of came to me as do most of my good ideas. I was down to the wire and sweating it. My California State Sample Ballot had finally cornered me with a little help from the US Postal Service. It lay on the coffee table, plastered in yellow change of address stickers. I'd moved a couple of times since registering to vote that year.

That Sample Ballot kept its virginity for about a week, spine unbroken. Finally, the night before Big Tuesday I cracked that motherfucker open. I couldn't believe it. I was lost in page after page of cheap newsprint that could have been a field repair manual for the AR-15, for all the sense it made to me. I mean, sure, it wasn't a presidential election year and all, but that motherfucker was as confusing as your first condom.

There were all these Propositions and Measures and Countermeasures that cross-referenced and negated each other until my brain shut down in a confused 'I don't know, so how can I make an informed decision much less give a fuck' kind of panic. Let me put it to you this way: it got real tiresome.

I didn't know what the fuck to do but one thing was sure: I didn't want to wade through all that election propaganda bullshit. So... here's where I confess my lameness. Not knowing what else to do, I called the Old Man.

This wasn't something I liked doing. Me and my father didn't talk much, let alone get along. I was living down south, going to school, and the only time I did call him was when I needed to borrow money, which I rarely if ever paid back. But let me tell you, I paid for it at the time because each check came with a fat lecture. Once again I was reminded that only a loser couldn't make ends meet and a man pays his own bills. So, needless to say, I only called the Old Man when I was down and out and desperate.

Anyway, there I was thinking twice about calling the Old Man for some electoral advice, and sure enough, he answers it on the third ring. I cursed myself once again for being weak enough to ask him for anything.

"Hello?" Always that weird, annoyed tone but I guessed that the Old Man hated talking on the phone, too.

"Hey, Pops, what's up?" I asked jokingly.

"Kent?" he always recognized my voice but never got the name right.

"Kurt," I stated just to get his goat.

"Yeah, I knew," he snapped, and then added, "What do you want?" suspiciously.

"Hey, I don't want anything," I answered defensively, because for once I really didn't want anything, except for maybe some of that electoral advice I was telling you about.

"I just wanted to see how you were doing," I added for maximum guiltage.

"Oh, pretty good," he started, confused. "The head of our department is retiring tomorrow and they're not hiring anyone to take his place due to budget cutbacks, so they're making us take up his slack."

It went on from there but that was pretty much the meat of it. I quickly lost interest and began wondering just who the hell they were and what gave them so much power over my Old Man. Finally, I cut in and got down to the nitty gritty.

"Hey, Pop, I was wondering. Who are you voting for?"

This set him off but I already had a pen and my Sample Ballot in hand. I cradled the phone with my head and shoulder and started taking notes. The Old Man was too engrossed with rattling off his own brand of twisted, paranoid logic that he failed to notice the silence coming from my end of the line.

I just muttered, "Uh huh," at the appropriate moments and tried to keep up.

Shit, I even asked his opinion on a couple of Measures that were on my ballot but not on his. That night I slept deep and sound (yeah, well, the eight beers I swilled after getting off the phone sure helped).

First thing in the morning I staggered into my designated polling place wiping the beer-laden sleep biscuits out of the corners of my eyes, pulled out my notes, and basically canceled the Old Man's ballot out.

Man, it felt great. I voted exactly opposite him Prop by Prop and Measure for Measure. Now that was democracy in action. My opinion meant enough to directly negate his. I couldn't believe my satisfaction as I stuffed my ballot into the box. I was now officially a man in Uncle Sam's eyes.

So basically, that's what I've been doing every two years since: calling the Old Man up, getting his opinion, then slamming the door in his face. It got me by, and maybe even almost made me look forward to, the coming elections. Well, this year the Old Man threw me a curve.

"Hey, Pops, what's up?" I asked as usual.

"Kent?"

"It's Kurt, Dad, ...Kurt," I half laughed and half sighed.

"I knew," he answered, as irritated as ever.

"Hey, man... Who are you voting for?" I asked around the pen in my mouth. I'd decided to cut to the chase, not wanting to waste any time on that damn phone.

"Oh, man..." This sounded like I pissed on his cornflakes.

It made me feel like a worthless piece of shit because the Old Man usually got so worked up. It was weird to hear him sound defeated. I pulled the pen out of my open mouth before it fell out.

"What about Bush?" I asked, trying the obvious.

"Are you kidding? Look at where we are now. That man is a criminal. He should be in jail along with his son Neil, not in the White House... And that Quayle is an idiot." The Old Man faltered, then started again slowly but picking up steam fast.

"Perot? Midget Nazi motherfucker. I wouldn't vote for him if he paid me and I wouldn't put it past him. That guy is psychotic." Damn, it didn't take much to get him going again.

"Clinton? I don't trust that slick motherfucker. He's a wannabe Kennedy for chrissakes and all he really is, is some deep south hick dumbshit."

It was great. I could just imagine the vein pounding in my Old Man's forehead as he clutched the phone and cursed into the receiver. I wondered if his new wife was witness to this.

"Basically, Kurt, they're all fucked," he summed it up. "I'd fuck 'em all over, somehow, if I could just find a way to do it."

Suddenly it came to him.

"Shit, I oughta just write my own name in for President. The rest of them can suck my dick. You know, that would be the proper 'Fuck You'. Just write in my own fucking name."

The Old Man stopped, puzzling it out. I begged off, saying my roommate needed to use the phone and hung up in shock. The Old

Man had finally lost it. Lost all faith in the American Electoral Process that he had invested so many years in. All that time and energy for nothing. His system had let him down and he knew it. It should have made me feel good, but to be honest with you, it just made me feel cheap.

Well, as usual, the next morning I staggered into my designated polling place and got ready to vote. But somehow it didn't seem right. I mean, what the fuck was I gonna do?

I stared down blankly at the empty ballot and then it came to me. Seemed so obvious and simple that I smiled and began marking my ballot. And you know what? I wrote my Old Man's name in for President.

The Paradise Lounge

I went to a poetry reading awhile ago at the Paradise Lounge. My friend Jim promised it was better than sitting home on a Sunday night watching TV, you know, being live entertainment and all. I was skeptical (not really thinking I was the poetry type), but the price was right: free. We decided to meet inside and check it out.

I remember thinking to myself as I walked in, "Poetry, huh? This should be pretty tame." But I'm here to tell you Bad Luck and Trouble follow me around like bored little brothers.

Anyway, I showed up about ten minutes late for the poetry reading, which was probably a good thing, meant I missed about ten minutes of it. Immediately, I noticed one thing about poets: they carry around way too much paper with them. You'd think that being educated, politically correct, poetry types they would try to conserve paper in these environmentally trying times and all, but no. Everyone had seven or eight sheets spread out in front of them like they were gonna break out in verse at any given moment.

Even from the back of the room, where I like to stand, I could hear people drop buzzwords like "tonality," "commitment," and "work-in-progress," in between names. Holy smokes, I knew I was in for a literate experience.

Well, it was obvious I was late because the featured Poet-Guy was already on. Now, I don't want to sound like some sort of a poetry snob or connoisseur or something (hell, my taste is in my mouth) but in my opinion this guy was no good.

He stood in the cliché Poet-Guy stance: one leg forward, weight on the back leg, head held slightly aloft, arm cocked - the whole nine yards. He even had on a turtleneck sweater. A white one. It grated my nerves to no end.

I mean, Poet-Guy was really full of himself. He had these insipid voices for the characters in his poems. I swear, well, actually to his credit, one of them sounded like Mr. Whoopee from the old *Tennessee Tuxedo* cartoon.

And worse yet, Poet-Guy kept mentioning his book over and over and over, like we were gonna rush out after the reading and buy it at our nearest all night bad poetry store. He started one poem with, "This is dedicated to the woman who published my book...," and another with, "This is from my book..." I consciously forgot the title.

Anyway, as if this wasn't enough, his poetry was loaded with these huge, obscure words. It got to the point where I couldn't figure out what the fuck Poet-Guy was talking about. I don't know, call me stupid, but "Vermilion cuneiform reptiles issue forth from my delineated mind," just didn't do anything for me.

In fact, it seemed to me that Poet-Guy was trying to demonstrate his mental superiority to the rest of us dim slobs. Like we should be jealous of his iron-fisted grasp on the English language. Several were the times Poet-Guy began on a lengthy, indecipherable, free-form tangent and I found my mind wander off to more immediate mundane thoughts:

Should I try to shoulder my way through the crowd at the bar for another beer?

Man, that girl across the room sure has on a stupid looking hat.

I hate the Poet-Guy's turtleneck sweater - needs a drink spilled on it.

You know, just those typical, random, bored type of thoughts that pop up unexpectedly as your eyes sweep the room. I guess the crowd felt the same way because they turned ugly. These three girls in the front had lost all interest and were talking among themselves, trying to drown out Poet-Guy. Regardless, he went on. The rest of the crowd began to heckle Poet-Guy. I couldn't believe it, because that seemed like a really fucked thing to do to someone who had the guts to stand up in front of a room full of strangers and read his bad poetry out loud, but I had to hand it to them; Poet-Guy deserved it.

"Yeah, yeah, yeah...," a girl to my left called out.

"It's got a point, right?" asked someone sarcastically.

I turned around and headed towards the bar for a beer.

"Wrap it up!" came a male voice behind me.

Poet-Guy must have taken the last heckler's advice seriously because he announced he was done. A couple of people in the crowd clapped distractedly as he gathered up his papers and walked off the little two-inch high stage. Turning from the bar, I was treated to a view of Poet-Guy storming up, as his bad-poetry-lovin' girlfriend ran over in awe.

She hugged him and said something to the effect of "You were great, honey," proudly in some unintelligible European accent.

Poet-Guy couldn't even be honest with himself. "It had its highs and lows," he answered.

I asked the bartender for a beer, feeling slightly sickened. Poet-Guy pushed his way up to the bar and ordered two conciliatory drinks, paying with the chips he had received in compensation for his performance. Being kind of curious as to what Poet-Guy was drinking, I hung around for a second at the bar. Brown liquor over ice in a couple of hefty-sized glasses. I went back to where a couple of friends of mine were standing.

Soon enough the next poet came on. They announced her as Terri White or Weiss or something like that, I didn't really catch her name but she was pretty good. At least she felt and meant everything she said, it wasn't just an exercise in mental masturbation meant to humiliate the rest of us. Terri was really into it and for that I respected her.

It worked well enough for the crowd because they quieted down. One of Terri's last poems was titled, 'Bike Messenger Leads The People,' or something like that but I'd already had a couple of beers by then.

Anyway, "Burn it down!" was her theme because she kept screaming it out every couple lines, her back arched, hands clenched, eyes screwed shut.

Suddenly, right in the middle of it, some asshole slurs out "Burn it down!" at the top of his lungs like some sort of drunken, tardy parrot.

"Oh well," I remember thinking, "the crowd grows restless again."

Another "Burn it down!" blurts out right behind me, and when I turn to see who it was spitting in my ear, lo and behold, it's the Poet-Guy. Only he must have sucked down those two huge doses of liquid courage because now he's Drunken-Angry-Poet-Guy.

I couldn't fucking believe it. He'd just gotten heckled off the stage and here Poet-Guy was doing the same thing to somebody else. I mean, if someone hurt you, why would you turn around and become just like them? I guess it was part of that If You Can't Beat 'Em, Join 'Em, spread-the-grief-around sort of mentality that I love so much.

So anyway, now I've got Drunken-Angry-Poet-Guy behind me, draped over his Euro-babe, hurling out abuse from the safety of the back of the room. Every time he screamed out some insult, they would lurch forward and stumble into me. Let me tell you, Euro-babe was digging it, giggling all the while.

After about the fifth time he had screamed out some stupid comment and they'd slammed into me, I was about to tell this dork, "Hey look, I ain't no Aladdin's Lamp. Quit rubbing up against me."

Well, right about then Terri announced she was finished and mercifully, Drunken-Angry-Poet-Guy fell silent.

After a ten minute break, it was open mike and people were

allowed to come up and read one poem each. They were about on par with the rest of the evening, some better than others. One thing bothered me though; everyone just walked up, meekly read their poetry and stepped off.

I couldn't see going out like that. If I was up there, I'd want to rattle their cages, tell the audience how much I hated nose rings, scream at them. Anything for a response other than that bored, polite smattering of applause. Anyway, at key moments in each poem the Drunken-Angry-Poet-Guy would offer his keen and witty insight. At least they seemed keen and witty to him but he was fucked up. And each time they would crash into me.

Finally, I turned around and considered punching him right in his fucking fat face. Wipe that smug grin right off his intellectually superior head. You know, spill a little blood on that virgin turtleneck sweater.

Well, about then this blonde in one of those trendy leopard skin pillbox type hats that are so hip nowadays, walked up to read her poem. It was this really twisted tale of growing up in an Italian-American family. All about her mother losing her virginity to a family relative, her own father's and brother's sexual advances, and the family's refusal to talk about any of it, all tied up in this crazy, shifting psycho-babble.

Drunken-Angry-Poet-Guy yelled out some pretty stupid shit but I was too lost in Twisted-Poetry-Girl's tragic childhood experiences to really notice. It was pretty cool, let me tell you. Afterwards, the crowd cheered - they like a little blood - and Twisted-Poetry-Girl walked off. Right then, this little old lady who was near me, exploded.

I mean to say she was irate, livid, hysterical, and three or four other adjectives I can't come up with at the moment, but mostly hysterical.

The Hysterical-Old-Lady was about forty-five or fifty, a shock of dark hair peppered with gray, glasses, maybe 4'11" and eighty pounds. Now the Hysterical-Old-Lady'd been sitting through two hours of bad poetry and had about all she could stand. She leapt up and screamed "Bigot!" into Twisted-Poetry-Girl's face as she tried to pass by.

Twisted-Poetry-Girl didn't know what the fuck to say to the Hysterical-Old-Lady who was blocking her path.

"Finally, confrontation," I thought to myself. Something I could really get into. It was great, I had front row seats and the events unfolded right before my very eyes.

The Hysterical-Old-Lady screamed "You bigot!" again and yanked Twisted-Poetry-Girl's poem out of her hands, wadded it up and threw it on the ground.

Twisted-Poetry-Girl's eyes bugged out. "...Hey look, lady, I was born into this," she finally managed to stammer.

"Every time I come here," the Hysterical-Old-Lady shrieked, " all I hear is bigotry." And with that she reached out and tore this string of trendy hippie beads from around Twisted-Poetry-Girl's neck.

"Fuck yeah!" I thought. "Let's beat up the poets!"

I turned around and looked for Drunken-Angry-Poet-Guy. This was it. I was going to punch him right in his fucking mouth. Get a couple of good shots in and maybe a kick or two while he was down. Teach him a good lesson about feeling superior and heckling people. Adrenaline OD.

Unfortunately, all I caught was a glimpse of Drunken-Angry-Poet-Guy's back as he and Euro-babe disappeared down the stairs. 'He who hesitates...' is the moral of that story.

Well, the best part of this whole sordid tale was, my friend Miles was on stage ready to do his thing, and during all the scuffling he kept repeating into the mike, "Excuse me, this is Poetry, not Performance Art, you'll have to leave."

So right on cue the bouncers came. Two huge Nirvanabe's with ponytails and leather jackets, but they didn't know what the fuck to do. How could they bounce the Hysterical-Old-Lady?

They tried to grab her arms to escort her out but that made the Hysterical-Old-Lady all the more hysterical. By then she was kicking, squirming and screaming. Shit, I didn't think anyone could get that wound up over bad poetry. Boy, was I wrong.

Finally, they got a grip on her and dragged the Hysterical-Old-Lady out. It was great. Definitely the climax to the show. In retrospect, it turned out to be a pretty cool evening and I got to see something pretty unexpected: violence at a poetry reading.

Another Night at the Paradise

As I've said before, I work the swing shift at my job and I don't get off until 11:00 p.m. so I'm usually up late. It's pretty cool because I'm able to check out anything that's going on but it also kind of sucks because amateur drunks aren't a pretty sight. I guess this is one of those stories.

I was about to split from work one night, not really in the best of moods when I got a call from my girlfriend Chase. Turned out a few of her friends had met down at the Paradise Lounge for some beers and they wanted to see if I wanted to catch up to them, in more ways than one. None of the guys from work wanted to come along but I paid it no nevermind. The ride over went without a hitch, even found a fairly legal parking spot not two blocks away. Well, lo and behold, that night seemed to be going my way because admission was free and I was able to find Chase and her small party of friends that had now grown to eight women, dressed up and revved up for a night out on the town. Linda was there, and Reginder, Ana, Kelley , Beth, Cindi - and two or three others that I can't remember their names right now and probably would be hard pressed to, even if they were standing in front of me buck naked.

Aw shit, I remember thinking to myself. This wasn't one of my preferred arrangements in which to have a couple of relaxed beers and unwind. You see, when the girls get together they tend to attract a crowd and a scene. Let me put it to you this way. It kind of puts me in an awkward position when, say you're at Du Nord and Giovanni the Margarita King and his entourage are telling your girlfriend and her friends how beautiful they are, and how they must come to his bar. I don't mean to complain, but jeez dude can't I come along?

Fortunately the Paradise was pretty dead that night so the girls had a couple of tables up on the balcony to themselves. I climbed the stairs, spotting Chase. She was caught in a conversation, the light from the pool room spilling out and illuminating half of her face as she spoke. It framed her profile, the smoke from a cigarette clutched in her hand snaking its way past her face. She looked beautiful as ever and I wanted to just stand there and watch her unobserved forever but she caught sight of me out of the corner of her eye. Chase smiled ignoring her end of the conversation that she was supposed to be holding up. I closed the distance between us as the rest of the girls recognized who it was.

"Kurtles!" they all called out, almost in unison. Don't even start me on that one.

"Hey ladies," I answered checking the group. I figured it was about the third round of drinks clutched in their fists by the look in their eyes. Not fucked up but on the road there. I knelt down next to Chase, "Hey."

She kissed my cheek and I felt myself blush not believing my luck.

"What's up?" I said trying to regain my composure. "Do you need a beer?"

"Yeah," Chase answered coyly, motioning with her almost empty.

"I'm going to the bar," I stated to the girls seated around me. "Anybody need anything?"

"Naw," seemed to be the consensus.

I walked through the pool room and to the back window of the upstairs bar. The bartender was busy dealing with what turned out to be a pretty large drink order so it took a couple of minutes to get to mine.

"Two Rolling Rocks, please," was it.

The bartender was kind as always so I left her a nice tip. Remember, if you want another drink without attitude always leave a tip. I gathered up my barley sodas and made my way back to the balcony. I was in for a surprise when I rounded the corner.

There he stood, crowding their table, beer in hand trying to throw a little rap. A white guy. Six feet tall, 180 pounds. I couldn't believe the outfit: a tan suede leather jacket with fringe hanging off the arms, black t-shirt stretched tight over his chest musculature, jeans perfectly faded and ripped in all the right places, black cowboy boots.

I focused on his face trying to figure out what was going on. Short dirty blond hair parted to the side, four days of facial stubble perfectly barbered (I always wondered what happened to all those 'Miami Device' razors they sold during the '80s), blue eyes. The guy would have been good looking if he wasn't so fucked up. I mean it was pretty obvious the Pick-up Artist was drunk as fuck: his eyes focused on that middle distance between him and whoever he was talking to, thousand yard stare stylee. His balance was off and what probably felt to him like a subtle shift in weight to make a point looked more like the uncoordinated lurching of someone who can't handle his sauce. That's when I caught a hint of what was going on.

"...so that's when I thought I'd come over and see what you girls are up to."

Oh shit, I thought. This ain't gonna be good. The girls weren't having any of the Pick-up Artist shtick and they were quick to let him know it.

"Hey look," one of them stated, "we're just here to have some drinks, okay? We're not here to meet a bunch of guys." Normally this would have chased even the boldest of suitors off, but as I said, blood was pretty fucked.

"I'm new to S.F.," the Pick-up Artist slurred on regardless. "I'm going to S.F. State and don't know many people."

With this, the girls' patience ran thin. "Look, guy," Linda cut to the chase. "We don't need this, we're just getting a drink. Can't you leave us alone?"

This seemed to get through the haze because the Pick-up Artist snapped like a dry twig.

"You know, you fucking West Coasters are all stuck up." He started yelling, "You think you're so fucking cool. I've been all over the world, you ain't so fucking cool. I've lived in Europe, I've been to the Far East, I've been around the world twice. You don't know shit."

All through the Pick-up Artist's tirade the girls were just tearing him apart.

"Dude, why don't you just keep on moving along?"

"We're not impressed."

"Yeah, yeah, yeah."

Well, I couldn't help but feel sorry for the Pick-up Artist so I came to his aid.

"Hey, you guys give the guy a break," I told the girls. "The guy is probably pretty tired. I mean with just getting off of a world tour and all."

This seemed to quiet everybody down for a second. The Pick-up Artist looked at me as if it was the first time that he had noticed the presence of another male in the crowd, which in his state he probably hadn't.

"Huh?" he asked.

"I mean, you are George Michaels, aren't you?" Well, I'd issued the challenge so now it was time to reap the rewards. I steeled myself for an exchange of taunts. I liked this game. Name the personality you most resemble. I mean I'd heard pretty much all of them at that point: "Funny Opera-Guy" or "Look who's talking, Kramer" or "Ha, ha, Guy from *Friends*," and I was looking forward to something new. Unfortunately, George Michaels took the easy way out.

"Fuck you," he began in his best Brooklyn accent which I must admit didn't sound too authentic. "I'm from New York," (I seriously doubted it), "I don't have to take this shit from some fucking West Coaster. I oughta kick your ass."

The girls were forgotten as George Michaels focused on his new found object of hatred, the cause of all his woes, the thorn in his side. Me.

"Fuck you," he reiterated moving so as to be right in my face. "You think you're so cool..."

I looked down at myself, checking out the goofy clothes I had on, wondering where he got that idea.

"... You wanna take it outside?"

"Look, dude," I emphasized the "dude" just to get his goat in a West Coaster, whatever the fuck that means, sort of way. "I was trying to help you out and this is the thanks I get?"

I was ready to let this thing pass but George Michaels wouldn't let it die.

"Fuck you. I'm gonna kick your ass. Let's go outside," he said, punctuated with a shove to my chest.

I had been drinking my beer calmly all along and held the empty. I guess that was it. George Michaels was threatening me and I'd had my ass kicked too many times before to let it happen again. I hate physical violence and all but with that shove I considered ending this whole thing. Here was some fucked-up dumbshit claiming New York, threatening me and trying to take it outside, and I really didn't want to hear anymore. George Michaels was so drunk he never would have seen it coming. The thrill of trying to kick a smaller guy's ass, the agony of an empty beer bottle hurled in your face.

I guess the girls sensed where this whole thing was going because they stood up all around us.

"You wanna fight, motherfucker?" Kelly screamed right in George Michaels' face.

"Fight us," Ana yelled.

This seemed to take the wind out of George Michaels' sails because he started to throw glances around him. Hell, it surprised the shit out of me.

"I'm sick of this shit," Reginder yelled. "Get the fuck out of here or we're gonna kick your ass."

The girls all yelled, "Yeah!" in unison.

Well, George Michaels took his cue and stormed of with a final "Fuck you." I couldn't believe it.

I felt like a complete idiot. Here a bunch of women had to save my ass, but I'll tell you the one thing that kept me from rocking his biscuit: I would need a few years and many thousand dollars of psychiatric therapy if I were to lose a fight to George Michaels.

Halloween

Let me start off by saying this: even though I think their music sucks, GWAR is one of my favorite bands and this is the reason why.

A couple of years ago, these friends of mine's band, MCM & The Monster, got a gig down at the Oasis (of all lame joints), for a Sunday night. The only redeeming factor of the whole thing was, since that Sunday night was Halloween and all, patrons arriving in costume got in free. That meant funds for an extra drink in my world, so I vowed to attend in character. Which character was my only problem.

Let me explain. I love Halloween and every year I try to be something more annoying than the year before. It's the only holiday I can really get into because it's the only day in the year that people get drunk and fall down costumed as the craziest shit and I'm usually right there to appreciate it. Being dressed as your favorite large American brewery's cartoon pitchman only enhances the surreality of one's experience.

So I've been for Halloween (not in chronological order, you know): Madonna, Captain Crunch, a priest, the Lucky Charms leprechaun, a frat boy, one of the Bay City Rollers, Colonel Sanders, anything. Shit, when I was a little kid, Speed Racer was my favorite. However, this year I was drawing a blank. It all seemed like it had been done before or wasn't thought out or was just plain lame. That's when a friend of mine made up my mind for me.

I'll call him Max because that's what his name is.

Now, Max had just recently been given a '67 Chevy Camaro by a good friend of his. Kathy (the generous friend) had mentioned that she had a car up for grabs and Max had been the only one bold enough to actually take her up on it. Kathy said no problem, all he had to do was come by and pick it up. If you think this sounds too good to be true, you're right, it was. So before you get any ideas about a bitchin' Camaro, let me describe this wreck.

Kathy said it was sitting in the driveway. She failed to mention that actually it was sitting in the driveway under a tree where it had been laid to rest three and a half years before. Apparently it had been Kathy's brother's once and he had gotten the bright idea to fashion his own convertible. This he effected with a large rock and a sawzall. The window posts seemed to go easy enough but he had a harder time with the roof where it was joined to the windshield. A jagged edge right at lobotomy level beckoned above your head. Even disregarding the stove-in rear left quarter panel, that car wasn't a pretty sight.

We surveyed the corpse buried under a four-inch thick layer of rotting leaves. At one time it must have originally been red or at least sprayed with red primer in patches but that had been faded and rusted by years of sitting dormant in the elements until it resembled a forgotten pair of pliers left out in the rain. We scraped the top layer of detritus off of the hood and windshield. I peered in through the grime. A stick shift, just like Kathy had said. I gave Max the thumbs up. He went to retrieve the spare gas can from my car while I bailed out the driver and passenger seats. Pillbugs and spiders galore.

Max returned with the can of gas. He dumped most into the tank and went around front to prime the carburetor. Kathy doubted that the Camaro would start but she lived at the top of a five block hill so we hoped for better. I sat in the driver seat as Max pushed me down and out of the driveway and into the street. I pointed the Camaro downhill and set the parking brake.

"It's your car," I said. "You wanna try it?"

Max replied, "Hell yeah," and I slid out of the door to push, hoping to add the critical amount of extra energy necessary to start that decaying beast. We got up to a running clip when I lost wind. They coasted away downhill while I coasted to a stop.

I screamed, "Hit it," just as Max did, punching it into first and dropping the clutch hard and fast. Lots of smoke and screeching tires but no fire because the Camaro almost came to a grinding halt without catching.

"Come on," I murmured in encouragement.

Max continued on down the hill and tried again with no success. He had already used up three of his five blocks and it looked like this might have been his last chance. He blew through the stop sign on the corner desperate for a little more speed. I watched in suspense, unconsciously flexing the muscles in my jaw. This was it.

Max popped the clutch, viciously stomping on the accelerator. To no avail. The Camaro quickly lost momentum bucking and shuddering and generally trying to tear itself apart. It sputtered almost to a stop and then miraculously caught.

I couldn't fucking believe it. I heard the engine roar as it spewed a pitch black, toxic cloud out of its tailpipe. Max gunned the motor savagely, in deep satisfaction. My feet were already carrying me down the hill at a rapid clip. Kathy was left in her driveway, forgotten.

"We outta here," I screamed as I caught up to the Camaro and vaulted in over the closed passenger side door.

Max turned and smiled.

"Yeah, boy," was his answer.

We went deep and long, cruising along Shattuck. The motor purred, occasionally backfiring and sputtering but otherwise chugging along like the diehard V8 workhorse Pride of Detroit it was. We passed a small knot of high school girls and they pointed and laughed as we went by so I knew we were t-rolling a fresh ride. The rotting leaves and small bugs flying into our eyes as we came up to speed were a little disconcerting, and we left a billowing trail of organic confetti in our wake, but otherwise it was a fine chariot.

Well, Max pimped that fresh load for about two weeks until the U-joint seized. Happened right in his driveway so there it sat for awhile under a new and different tree than the last. I guess that Camaro preferred a shady spot for its final resting place. Not soon after, Kathy's boyfriend John-boy called Max up. At first he hemmed and hawed about what's up and all that, but he got right down to the meat soon enough.

"Hey, Max," John-boy asked, "what's up with the Camaro?"

"Nothing," Max answered suspiciously. "What's up?"

John-boy explained that he had a pre-Halloween party to go to on Saturday night and he was thinking about getting a bunch of his friends together and going as Batman. Now this was a couple of years before Tim Burton's tough-guy movie *Batman* came out so he was talking about the '60s, campy, TV Batman. John-boy figured he had all the main characters covered. In fact, he invited Max to join the festivities as Mr. Freeze. I had to give it to John-boy, Lord Large would have made a great Mr. Freeze. Max declined the offer but assented to loan out the Camaro considering its fucked-up state.

True to his word, John-boy came over a few days later and, using a hammer and a two-by-four, pounded the U-joint back into shape. That's when the real fun started. He had also brought a couple of cardboard boxes, a roll of duct tape, and two cans of flat black spraypaint. I picked up the duct tape trying to puzzle out its use.

With it and the cardboard boxes, he fashioned huge cartoon fins on the rear quarter panels. I had to admit that they looked pretty good, considering. From there, John-boy proceeded to apply one thick, runny and dripping in spots, coat of flat black spraypaint. After drying, red masking tape was applied as pin striping and a gold bat was stenciled on the doors to make the image complete. Hell, we even bolted on a plastic tub on the rear below the trunk, painted to resemble the Batmobile's jet booster. We stepped back to admire our work.

"She's all yours," was all Max could think of to say, handing John-boy the keys.

John-boy patched out in the driveway, leaving us to choke on his cloud of thick, black, oily exhaust. He looked like some insane, broken down, tortured futuristic vision of the campy '60s Batmobile from hell. Pretty cool, let me tell you. I laughed and punched Max in the arm as we went up the stairs to his apartment.

"Don't punch me, man," was his answer.

"Man, you shoulda gone as Mr. Freeze with those guys. Looks like it would be hella fun."

Max just gave me a rare look like he was above all that.

I went to a party that night but not dressed as anything. I guess I'm a purist or something but somehow it doesn't feel right to be in costume on the night before Halloween. Sure, get drunk and warm up for the big night and all, but save the costume shit for Halloween. That's what it's for.

Halloween morning found me pretty hungover and not much closer as to making a decision in the way of a costume for that evening. I limped over to Max's cradling my aching brain. A couple of loads later I was feeling a little bit better. That's when the phone call came.

"John-boy," Max called out into the receiver. "What's up?"

I eavesdropped wondering how their evening went. From what I could make out, there were about eight of them: from Batman and Robin, to Catwoman and Batgirl, to the Penguin and Riddler. They hit up three different parties and tore shit up wherever they went. Sounded like they had a good time - no drunken altercations or unsolicited DUIs. John-boy promised to bring the Batmobile back to Max in a couple of minutes.

He wasn't kidding because a couple of minutes later we heard the high pitched whine of powersteering belts slipping, followed by a car bottoming out in the driveway.

"John-boy must be here," I stated the obvious from my spot on the couch.

We looked out the window to see John-boy vault out of the driver's seat. He cupped his hands together and yelled "Max!" up at the front deck. Max got off the couch and headed out the front door. I followed.

"What's up?" Max yelled down, in a huff.

"I gotta go and pick up my kid," John-boy yelled back.

Max started down the stairs, shaking the entire staircase. I went down after the shuddering stopped, not wanting to be involved in the destruction. I hit ground just as John-boy handed off the keys.

"Yeah, man, I gotta pick up my kid and do the family thing tonight," he explained.

"Man, that sucks," I commiserated. "The Monster is playing tonight."

John-boy asked where and when, and I filled him in on the details.

"Whatcha gonna be?" he asked.

"I don't know," I mumbled, looking down in defeat. We stood there for a second, lamely.

"Hey, you could be Batman if you want," he offered. "I'm just gonna take my kid trick-or-treating tonight. I'm not using it."

I thought about it for a second, weighing my options.

"Fuck yeah!" I answered, sealing my fate.

A car horn honked from the street out front of Max's. From the way John-boy looked at us I could tell it could only be his girlfriend.

"I gotta go, but come by my house in an hour or so," he promised. We watched him hustle down the driveway.

"You aren't really gonna go see The Monster dressed as Batman, are you?" Max asked incredulously.

"Fuck yeah!" I repeated myself for emphasis.

I went home soon after that, but on the way I stopped by John-boy's. His son Josh was tearing the apartment up as usual when he visited. He was pushing a Tonka firetruck around the living room and making siren noises at the top of his lungs.

"Hey, Josh, what's up?" I called out. He ignored me. John-boy laughed and let me in the door. "Sounds like you guys had fun last night."

"Yeah man, it was killer," was his reply. "I got most of the pieces together," he offered, motioning to a heap of blue material on the couch.

I started picking through it. There was, in order: one blue pair of women's tights size XL; a men's black Speedo bathing suit size 36; a black t-shirt with the same Bat logo and in the same gold spray paint as was sprayed on the doors of the Batmobile; a blue mid-length cape; a black mask complete with thin piece of elastic across the back; blue rubber dishwashing gloves; and an old yellow plastic toy belt that had been Josh's once. It was broken and had been fixed with duct tape to simulate Batman's utility belt. I was laughing just going through the pile.

"The only thing I can't loan you is the shoes," John-boy explained motioning down towards the pair of blue Converse All-Stars on his feet. "Cause I'm wearing 'em."

I thanked him, not really wanting to wear his shoes anyway, and let myself out of his front door. The ride back to my house went off without a hitch.

Around seven o'clock, I gave Max a call to suggest we T-roll the Batmobile over the bridge. He agreed, still not believing I was going as Batman. I told him I would be right over. I grabbed the bag with John-boy's costume in it and headed over. Got sidetracked getting a 40-ouncer of Mickey's on the way, but that was all right.

I knocked on Max's door and then let myself in. He was sitting on the couch, TV blaring, just like I had left him.

"What's up?" I asked, waving the bag full of Batman at him.

Max scowled. "I talked to Miles awhile ago. They're down at the Oasis doing soundcheck," he explained. "They said they'd meet us there."

I cracked open the 40 and took a long pull.

"Max," I asked, eyeing him, "have you figured out what you're gonna be yet?"

Max stared off, kind of scanning the room. His eyes focused on this cheap piÈata a friend had brought him from Guatemala for his birthday that was fashioned in the image of Mickey Mouse but more resembled Mickey Rat.

"Hadn't really thought of it," he mumbled.

"I don't know about you," I stated, referring to the Oasis, "but I'm getting in for free."

That seemed to carry some weight with Max because he considered the situation. I sucked on my Mickey's. It was draining a little faster than I would have preferred, but don't they always. I got down to the last third within three commercial breaks, long before Max could come to a decision.

"Hey, man," I said. "I'm gonna piss and then cut outta here. You gonna be ready?"

"Just take a piss," was his reply.

I did and when I got out of the bathroom, to my surprise, Max was no longer rooted to the couch. From the noise coming out of his bedroom I could tell he was rooting around in his dirty laundry pile. The thought of that made me shudder. I took my seat back on the couch. Figured it was time to put on the Batman costume and finish my 40. Max shuffled out of his bedroom, wearing black Levi's and a black t-shirt just as I was pulling on the blue tights. He carried a pair of black wingtips in his hand. I looked at him questioningly.

"I'm gonna be a mouse," he stated.

I couldn't help but laugh at him. I doubled over on the couch thinking about the biggest, baldest rat you'd ever seen in your life. It wasn't until he got out the scissors that I knew he was serious. I laughed even harder as I watched him cut the top of his Guatemalan pinata birthday present's head off. He was careful to cut around the giant cartoon mouse ears, fashioning a crude skull cap.

I was in hysterics at this point. I calmed down as he searched the apartment for a rubber band. He cut it open and duct-taped either end of the rubber band into the underside of the ears making a chin strap so as to strap the whole thing on his head. He slipped the ears on. I couldn't take it, breaking out into laughter again.

"Look," Max hissed, getting pissed off, "it's just until I get in."

I felt kind of stupid, not having that option, but continued suiting up. I pulled on the Speedo, slipped into my pair of black Nike high tops, tied the cape around my shoulders, duct-taped the yellow plastic toy utility belt around my waist, pulled on the blue rubber dishwashing gloves, and shoved the mask on my head. Transformation complete. I was now Batman, dammit. I looked into Max's bathroom mirror and I had to admit I looked pretty silly. I laughed, figuring what the fuck.

"We outta here," I stated to Max as I came out of the bathroom.

Max took one look at me and couldn't help but laugh himself. His laughter had a cruel edge to it. Made me want to change back into my civvies, but I wasn't going out like that.

"Let's go," was all I could say.

I made it down the stairs first because Max had to pause long enough to lock the door, and jumped into the driver's seat of the Batmobile. Somehow it just felt right. I laughed to myself until Max threw the keys down from the second landing onto the hood. They bounced with a loud jangle, coming to rest in the top grill. I stood and reached over the windshield for them, careful not to lay myself open on the jagged metal edge.

By the time I got the keys, Max was letting himself in through the passenger door. I sat back down, rammed the ignition key home and gunned it. The engine caught on the fourteenth or fifteenth crank, sounding like it never would. I threw Max a look but he just shrugged. We eased out of his driveway.

Well, we made it to the tollbooth at the Bay Bridge, no problem. That's when my troubles started. It took me a couple of seconds to get my wallet out of my tights, where I had tucked it for safekeeping. Meanwhile, carloads of people pulled by screaming out insults at Batman.

"Batman...Da na na na na na...Batman!"

"Hey, Batman... Where's Robin?"

You know, those kind of intelligent observations. Batman did not care for it one bit. I paid my toll and took off.

We were rolling down the Ninth Street exit off 101 in no time. I took the corner at 11th and there, up a block ahead, was The Oasis. I could see the line to get in from there. It was about twenty-five people deep.

About ten of them screamed out "Batman!" as we went by but I ignored them and concentrated on finding a parking space instead. One was had within the block which was strange considering the size of the Batmobile, but then again, it was Sunday after all. I turned the engine off and handed Max the keys since he had pockets, and the thought of walking around all night with someone's car keys jammed in my tights didn't really do anything for me. We walked up to the Oasis.

"Batman," the Bouncer motioned me around the crowd. "Go right in."

"Now that's how it should be," I told him.

"Cool car," he laughed around his tough-guy, bouncer face. The bouncer eyed Max's get-up but didn't say anything as he followed me in.

Inside it was kind of dead but filling up quick. I noticed about half of the crowd was in costume. This was an ominous sign but I looked forward to heaping some abuse on the apathetic ones. Maybe try to guess what they had inadvertently dressed as. First things first, I spied the downstairs bar and started making my way over.

"Hey, Batman," the bartender called out. "What can I get you?"

I better get used to this, I thought. "A Rolling Rock, please."

He brought my beer with a flourish. "Cool costume."

I tipped him a buck just for the support. Max ordered a beer for himself which was unusual, not being a big drinker anymore. I gave him a look but didn't say anything. Instead, I turned my attention to the crowd, hoping to locate Miles or Carol or Hector or Gary, or any of the guys in the band, for that matter.

"Let's see if we can find anyone," I offered the mouse standing next to me.

We started making our way towards the stage. I caught sight

of Miles out of the corner of my eye. He was over by a side of the stage talking to Carol and some girl I had never seen before. We strolled up. Neither Miles nor Carol were in costume, hating that shit.

"Hey, what's up?" I called out from beneath the mask.

Miles looked over with a blank stare of unrecognition.

"Miles...," I tried again.

"Kurt!" he exploded. "Jesus Christ!"

I stepped back to let him take a look.

"You look great," Carol screamed.

We all had a good laugh at my expense. I asked about the line-up that night. Evidently there was no opening band. The Monster was expected to do an extra long set and then some band from Virginia named GWAR was gonna play.

"Ever heard of them?" asked Miles.

I told him that I hadn't, and Miles filled me in on what he did know. Apparently GWAR had to headline because there just wasn't any going on after them. Something about costumes and fake blood and the stage getting trashed, but the management wasn't being specific.

Miles just shrugged and said, "All I know is that we're opening for them."

From there, the drinking began. We had staked out our area by the stage and pretty much stuck to it, occasionally sending out a scout to retrieve some grog. After awhile the stage manager motioned Miles over, indicating that it was time to perform. Miles looked over at us and shrugged. We watched him and the rest of the knuckleheads as they went backstage to load the equipment on.

I must say the band played pretty good, saving falling apart in drunken pieces until the end of their set. The crowd gave them a good response, clapping loud and long. I watched the guys break down their gear from the safety of the audience with Max and Carol. Batman does not roady out amps.

I noticed Max had ditched the mouse ears, so I now had extra ammo to heckle him with.

"Hey, Mouse-boy," I asked sweetly, "how's about getting me a beer?"

"Fuck you," came his answer.

Right about then, GWAR came on and broke into their intro number. Well, "costumes and fake blood" - they weren't kidding. Out came these costumed freaks like the hybridized bastard sons of a cheap Japanese video game mated with a grade-B horror movie come to life. All foam rubber scales and armor and muscles, fake blood, screaming guitars. It was all right, let me tell you.

I decided, however, that I desperately needed a beer to check out their set over. Without asking, I began shouldering my way back towards the bar.

"Hey, Batman," the bartender repeated himself, "what can I get you?"

"Three Rolling Rocks, please," I answered, figuring I'd get Max and Carol one while I was up. Miles got 'em free while on stage.

The bartender brought 'em and I paid. Even left a tip. Making my way back through the crowd was another matter. I kept getting bumped and almost lost a beer twice. Carol saw me coming.

"Let me get that," she said, taking her beer.

I motioned to Max with the other but he just shook his head. "I don't want a beer," he answered, all huffy.

I didn't pay it no nevermind because fuck it, and besides that, it meant that I now had two beers instead of just the one. That was A-Okay with me. I sucked at the bottle in my right fist, not noticing whose foot I was stepping on behind me. I felt a set of toes under mine and got off them as fast as I could.

"Sorry about that," I apologized over the music, half turning my head.

"Kurt Zapata?" came a female voice most unexpected like.

I turned to see who it was that could ID me that quick. And much to my horror, I realized that it was Julia Harris.

Julia was a girl I used to go out with when I was going to college. We were together one long and drug-addled summer when I was nineteen. Well, sure enough, as soon as I left to go back down to school, things went sour between us. I left without saying goodbye. She wouldn't return my calls. All that petty shit. I found out months later from a mutual friend that she started seeing someone else right after I left. I was pretty bummed out at the time but didn't blame her. Nevertheless, there she was standing in front of me.

She gave me the once over twice, stopping at the pair of matching beer bottles clutched in my fists, and said it again as if she couldn't believe the words, "Kurt Zapata?"

I could almost forget that I was dressed like Batman. I could almost forget that I looked like an idiot. Almost.

"Julia Harris," I answered, feeling myself blush. I could have killed myself at that moment for wearing that stupid Batman costume. She leaned back on her heels and gave me a smirk, feeling on top of the situation.

"Batman, huh?"

"Batman," I said in defiance, not giving her the satisfaction.

We stood looking at each other not knowing what to say. Sure, I had thought about that moment a few times, what I would say, what she would say, but now I was drawing a blank. I never foresaw bumping into her again dressed as Batman.

Well, I wanted to tell her that she had gotten to me or that I was cool or anything, but by the way she was looking at me, all I really wanted to tell her was that she was a bitch. It was a look of amused embarrassment. Or maybe it was a look of just downright embarrassment. All I know is that it really irked my ire.

"Hey," I tried to sound as genuine as possible. "Nice seein' ya."

I turned around figuring that I would ignore her. Seemed like the best course of action. Ignore 'em and they'll go away. I could feel her eyes lasering daggers into my back. Made my flesh crawl. I could just imagine her belittling me to her friends. "You shoulda seen him, he was dressed as Batman."

I was too busy obsessing on Julia that I almost failed to pay attention to the shenanigans going on about the stage. An Elvis imitator had come on stage with a huge styrofoam/foam rubber black ducktail stunt hairdo. The band members tore his head open and scooped out a bloody mouthful of brains each. This brought screams of approval from the audience.

Then a guy came out with a giant papier-maché/foam rubber penis strapped around his waist. I mean this thing was anatomically correct. And huge. So big that he had to support it with one hand. Well, he kept this hand busy stroking this veiny, hideous beast. Great attention to detail, let me tell you. I caught the motion out of the corner of my eye just at that magic moment.

He arched his back and, lo and behold, came.

I mean to say that the giant papier-maché/foam rubber penis began to spew forth fake jizz. I'm not talking about a little semen dribbling out of the tip. I'm talking about huge arcing ropes of love spurting out into the audience. In fact, just in time, I radared a fist-sized glob flying at my head. At the last moment I instinctively ducked and twisted out of its way.

Well, the person right behind me wasn't that lucky and, you guessed who it was. Julia.

She got hit dead center in the chest with that flying gob of spooey. It spattered her with a viscous plop. I turned just in time to see Julia react in horrified surprise, all frown. I almost fell down into the mire of spilled beer and fake semen on the floor, I was laughing so hard. I twisted my head around just in time to be treated to one last vision of Julia storming off in disgust. That was definitely the highlight of the night - I mean to say that it just doesn't get much better than that.

So that's why GWAR is my favorite band and Halloween is my favorite holiday. I'm not sure what I'm going to be this year either, but you know, I'm really looking forward to finding out.

Party

I went to a party. I wasn't invited and didn't know the couple throwing it, but that's never stopped me before. Gary, this guy I used to go to college with, threw down the 411 and clued me into the goings-on. I'd met Gary in the dorms.

His name was Gary Boldstein but we called him 'Gary Godhead' or just 'Godhead', for short. Godhead was about 5'7", short bristly dark brown hair, freckles, prominent nose. Otherwise nothing to really sit up and take notice over. His most memorable trait became obvious when he opened his mouth - pure comedy billowed forth. Gary was the most obnoxious person I knew, with the possible exception of his roommate at the time, but that was another story.

It didn't take much to set Godhead off onto some lengthy tangent that never failed to make me laugh. I was never sure if he just made this shit up free-form stream of consciousness style, or if he actually spent time thinking it up.

I mean, for the longest time Godhead was obsessed with forming an all bass band. You know: lead bass, rhythm bass, bass, bass drum and a baritone singer. We never agreed whether or not to include a horn section but he thought the addition of tuba, trombone, and baritone sax would give the resulting music a complex layered texture only enhancing the auditory experience. Shit, he even wanted kettle drum and church organ accompaniment. Maybe a foghorn would be nice. My boy thought big.

My argument was this: resonant frequencies tend to cancel each other out, so too many low end vibrations would create a muffled sound detrimental to fine audio quality. We did agree on one thing, however. It had the potential to go over big amongst the thumping stereo mini-truck wannabe thug types.

Anyway, Godhead's homeboy from the big law firm Pompous, Arrogant and Asshole where they slaved downtown at, had just moved in with one of the secretary/receptionist types. They were throwing a little housewarming party. Chips, dip, records, maybe two single women. You know, the usual boring shit. Godhead and a couple of his work-pals were going to barge the festivities and I was welcome to tag along fifth wheel style.

I told him, "Hell, yeah." Maybe I can find some rich attorney-babe who wants to go slumming, was my line of reasoning. You know, someone to show the cheap side of life to. Besides, odds were they were bound to have a killer snack tray. Get over on some serious grazing.

I hadn't bothered to eat anything all day. The emptiness was burning a hole in my stomach, being way past the point of hunger and well into nausea. I was going to pick up a bite to eat for dinner on the way home but somehow the thought of a piroshki from the corner liquor store didn't butter my biscuit. Whoever came up with the idea of a deep-fried meat and cheese filled doughnut was one sick motherfucker.

It was eight o'clock on the nose when they rang the buzzer to my apartment. I was about to get into the shower, naked, towel around my waist. The phone had just rung but I let the answering machine get it, not feeling like talking to anyone right at that second. Good instincts. It was some goofy girl for one of my roommates.

I had just gotten back from a fruitless trip to one of my favorite thrift stores, Clothes Contact, in the Mission. I knew it as 'Clothing by the Pound' because of the sign behind the cash register. What a cool concept - vintage clothing sold by weight. You could score some killer shit down there but you had to stick to the light fabrics: cotton, blends, some wools, or else it was gonna cost you. I saw a pea coat I liked but it weighed at least six pounds, and I didn't want to fork over that kind of cash for navy surplus. No short sleeved uniform shirts. I spent a whole fucking Saturday shopping for clothes and still didn't find a thing. Pretty frustrating. Did score a fresh ballcap earlier on, though.

I started my ill fated shopping spree at Kaplan's Discount Sporting Goods down on Market Street at about two in the afternoon, checking out the baseball hats. I had just gotten up with one of my patented near death experience hangovers. A real good one. My stomach kicked me awake, head three sizes too big. All I wanted was something to keep the sun out of my burning eyeballs.

Kaplan's was recommended to me by a friend for their veritable cornucopia of caps. I was not disappointed when I walked in through the front doors. The right hand wall of shelves was stacked to the roof with an assortment of insignias. I stood there dumbfounded, staring for a couple of minutes.

Man, they stocked all the professional sports teams you could think of and most of the big college ones. I opted for a Cleveland Indians ball cap, size 7-1/4 (being a pinhead and all). One of the killer all wool ones - no snaps or plastic shit in the back.

Don't get me wrong, I'm not a big Cleveland fan. Baseball is pretty fucking boring. I just liked the logo, a smiling Indian. Hell, they were even on sale. I think it was one of those reducing inventory, 'get rid of the dogs' sort of things because the box with the Indians' hats in it was way up high on a top shelf and pretty dusty. I left Kaplan's with the cap on my head and a smile on my face.

That was until some Joe Average-Guy walked by and said, "An Indians fan. You are all right."

Now, two things bothered me about this statement:

1) Sure I'm an Indians fan, but not the Cleveland Indians, you know what I mean? I'd like to see my boys come from the basement, clean house and take the league. But judging from statistics (and statistics don't lie, they're just easily manipulated), they're a dark horse. The Indians could use a ton of younger talent and some bigger hitters. They also needed to learn better cooperation between their players but I'm behind them all the way. The game ain't over yet, motherfuckers; and

2) Who the fuck was this guy to tell me I was or wasn't "all right"? I resented the fact that he would judge me solely by my stupid hat and felt compelled to hand down his little insights. Shut the fuck up, bitch. Who asked you?

Anyway, I strolled down Market Street feeling a real good attitude coming on. One of those 'get outta my way before I snap like a dry twig' sort of moods. I should have told that asshole to mind his own fucking business, but somehow it never occurs to me at the time. I was too surprised that some fuckhead felt obligated to give me his two cents worth. Hindsight is useless. If I let some idiot like that drag me down, I'm the one with the problem.

I got on the subway to go from Market to Clothing by the Pound in the Mission and sat in a seat next to the doors. I liked having the option of jumping off the train at any given stop. Kind of like an escape clause. I knew you were supposed to leave those seats for the elderly and handicapped but I sat there anyway. On the offhand chance that any elderly or handicapped individuals do happen to board this train, I will relinquish this seat to them promptly, I promised myself benevolently.

I looked around the train. The car was about half full of bored riders. They sat looking at their reflections in the dark windows or down at a shred of discarded newspaper clutched in withered hands. Hands that had spent a lifetime balled into fists without ever hitting anything. A couple were arguing in hushed voices, their angry murmurs floating down the aisle.

I think compulsory public transportation attendance should be the law of the land. The occasional bus, subway or train ride would be mandatory. Get face to face with the man on the street. You know, cheek to jowl with the Average Joe. I was fascinated with people, and every trip on public trani was a lesson in Humanity 101.

What makes people behave the way the way they do? I had kept my eyes open for twenty-seven years but was no more closer to an understanding than day one. Take for example, said subway ride from downtown to the Mission.

Across from me sat a mother and her two children. Classic white trash family unit. She was over thirty-five, bleached blonde hair, pear-shaped, and most nattily dressed, I might add, in some of K-Mart's best polyester slacks. The oldest kid was a small dark haired boy of about four, dressed in Toughskin jeans, little Converse Chuck Taylors and a hand-me-down looking sweater.

I couldn't distinguish the gender of the younger one. Just an eighteen-month-old tot in tiny light blue sweats and a red jacket. That poor little sucker had a halo of golden curls surrounding its cherubic li'l face. Maybe it's a boy and they're just waiting to give him his first haircut, I thought.

Anyway, their mother had obviously just purchased them a nutritious lunch. Each of those li'l ankle-biters clutched a corndog in one of their chubby li'l fists. I don't know what she was thinking, but each breaded and deep fried pork product was adorned with a single stripe of ketchup. Ketchup! Any idiot knows mustard is the condiment of choice for a corndog. The question in my head screamed, Who the fuck would eat a corndog topped with ketchup?

Apparently nobody, because those two just weren't going for it. The oldest sat there sullenly clutching the corndog stick, refusing to take a bite, despite his mother's constant whining. The other one was the hottest. Curls just got up and tottered around the aisle. I couldn't figure it out but it looked like the li'l rug-rat was searching for something.

Right before my stop, the kid wobbles over, sticks the barely gnawed upon, soggy corndog in my face and starts repeating, "Gah-bage, gah-bage," over and over.

Damn, I was surprised. That kid was fucking astute. Less than two years old and the li'l ankle-biter already realized that kind of deep fried fast food was no good for you. One of its first words and already calling bullshit. I got off the train feeling like maybe there was some hope for the world after all. That was until my bus ride back to the pad from Clothing by the Pound.

I got on to the bus and sat in one of the only available seats, near the front. Directly across from me was perched a middle-aged business man in a gray tweed jacket, dark blue slacks, white shirt, and red power tie. He was reading a *Chronicle*, I noticed as the doors closed. It was then that the BUS RIDE TO HELL began.

I couldn't help but stare at Business Guy, being right in the center of my field of vision. Homeboy obviously had a cold because every couple of seconds he would pause long enough in his reading to snort the mucus running out of his nose back up into his head.

Now, I'm not talking about a li'l sniffle meant to stem the tide, that would have been cool. But no, he really got into it. Each episode was a long, loud, gurgling honk accompanied by an audible swallow.

I had two questions: 1) Why wasn't there a word to describe that sick fucking action? Some sort of verb that could convey my disgust. I mean, even 'feltching' has a name.

And secondly, why didn't Mr. Power-Tie-Business-Guy have something to blow his nose on?

Shit, I had an old blue bandanna for just such an emergency. Even the lowliest derelict dying in an abandoned doorway on Market Street had a rag to wipe the drool from his chin. Mr. Power-Tie-Business-Guy, it seemed, couldn't afford one because he just sat there reading his newspaper and sucking the snot back up into his head. I was going to rip the tail of my shirt off and hand it to him so he'd stop. It made me sick just being near him and I didn't even have a cold yet, but that wasn't the worst part.

After a few minutes of this snort-fest, which seemed like a couple of eternities, the sneezing started. In between every four or five swallows he would let out a huge sneeze. I want to emphasize 'huge' because Mr. Power-Tie-Business-Guy wouldn't bother to cover his face. Only lower the paper. A giant cloud of virus laden snot/saliva mist billowed from his nose and mouth at me from across the aisle.

How long can I hold my breath? The question beat itself against the inside of my skull, looking for a way out, and we had only gone a couple of blocks.

Did he feel driven to share his disease with me? Like I should be grateful to receive anything from him, including the flu. You would think that an upwardly mobile, well bred kind of fella would exhibit some manners, common courtesy or restraint, but no. These rich types were the most self-centered, thoughtless motherfuckers on earth. I felt like punching him right in his red, runny nose and the only thing holding me back was the fact that I would be the one to go to jail.

'YOUTH ARRESTED IN PUBLIC TRANSIT CONFRON-TATION', the front page headline in that night's *Examiner* would have read.

What was I talking about? 'YOUTH SHOT BY POLICE IN BUS ATTACK', the small article on page C-17 underneath the obituary column would have begun.

I got off the bus in front of my place grinding my teeth in frustration. The bus pulled away from the curb leaving me to choke on its exhaust. I hated the thought of going all the way down to Clothing by the Pound, sifting through a bunch of moldy smelling old clothes and not even finding anything good like a golf jacket or a plaid pair of Bermuda shorts, something really tacky. To make matters worse, I had to brave Typhoid Mary Business-Guy on the way back to the house. I did, however, get a good laugh out of the velour Kennington shirts I found down at Clothing by the Pound. Reminded me of some of the crap my Mom tried to get me to wear in sixth grade: strictly cornball-o-rama, two-tone, fuzzy, '70s shit.

The buzzer rang for the third time, snapping me out of my daze. I couldn't believe that Godhead and his entourage were already here. The party didn't start until 8:30 and Gary said they would be by after 8. Meant 9 to me. I buzzed them in. They came up the stairs. I could hear their apprehensive footsteps echo up the stairwell as I unlocked the front door and poked my head out. Godhead rounded the last corner of the stairwell first.

"Hey, hey, Gary Godhead," I called out as his head appeared. "What's shaking?"

"You aren't ready yet," was all he could think of to say, which he did, unfortunately. Godhead was dressed in black slacks, navy blue sweater, and black penny loafers.

"I was just getting into the shower," I answered truthfully, truthfully annoyed. I left the front door to the apartment open and started walking down the hall towards the bathroom. I heard the rest of them reach the front door and stop cold in their tracks.

"This is it," Gary said over his shoulder to reassure his companions. They timidly stepped into the hall and shut the front door.

"I'm gonna take a shower," I called out before slamming the bathroom door. "TV's on, beer's in the fridge."

I undid the knot around my waist and let the towel fall to the floor. The linoleum felt cold under my feet. I dialed on the hot water. Pissed in the toilet while I waited for the shower to heat up. It was a pretty good one. Steam rose from the tub as my stream trickled to an end. I stepped through the shower curtains and scalded the fuck out of my chest with hot water. Frantically spinning the cold water knob only made it worse. Finally the shower cooled off a bit.

Shampooed, washed my face and body, then conditioned, all in that order. It was almost like a ritual. I stepped out of the shower before six minutes could elapse. A warm shower almost made me feel human again. I wrapped the towel around my waist and kicked open the door. A cloud of steam wafted out as I let loose a loud contented sigh. No response.

I could see into the living room as I stepped into the hall. They were watching MTV. The newest George Michaels video was on. Gary made a wisecrack about fashion victims. The other three eyed the screen hungrily as the camera flashed on each model, muttering their approval. They were transfixed with the occasional glimpse of female flesh captured on film. Ironically the song had something to do with freedom. It was pathetic. I noticed they hadn't even gotten into the beer yet. Some things were important, goddammit.

"You guys want a beer?" I called out as I tiptoed into the kitchen.

This rattled their collective cage because they stood in unison, mumbling their affirmation. Probably embarrassed by what they were thinking.

"Don't worry, it's written all over your faces." I yanked open the refrigerator door as they crowded their way into the kitchen, following Gary like little lambs. They stood in a nervous cluster-fuck near the door. I stared at them for a couple of tense seconds. Can't you idiots do anything without following someone? My unvoiced question hung in the air.

I reached down into the refrigerator and began handing out bottles, Godhead first. The water dripped off me, pooling up on the floor. Gary introduced each guy as they grabbed for their beers. Their names went in the old proverbial one ear and out the other, not really making much of an impression. Three seconds later and I couldn't have told you their first names if my life depended on it.

They seemed hesitant to shake mitts with a naked man clutching a frayed towel around his waist. I stuck my hand out to each of them anyway. It was kind of amusing to watch them squirm. I gave them each a little nickname as they finally reached for my outstretched damp palm.

Curly was the shortest of the three. I called him that because of the tangle of brown ringlets on top of his head. Not quite an afro but the white man's equivalent. Curly was about 5'4" and carried himself like he was suffering from an acute case of Little Man's Complex. Puffed out chest, slight swagger, like a Keebler Elf with attitude. He gave me a firm handshake, almost like a challenge. I kind of liked him. At least he was up front.

Godhead moved on to the next one. Dirty blonde hair, cut

short on the sides and left long in front so it hung in his eyes. Shit, he was hiding behind his bangs. Slim build, glasses, cherubic face. Radar might have been the youngest of the lot but it was hard to tell. He could have been anywhere from nineteen to twenty-nine years old. Total Gerber Baby face. Looked like he had a pretty trouble-free life. No visible scars or worry lines, generic clothes. Fucking mama's boy. Radar didn't say anything when we were introduced and wouldn't look me in the eye as we shook hands. I hated when people did that, it was real unfriendly. He even refused the beer I offered with a shake of his head.

"What's the matter?" my eyes asked. "Too good?"

The last guy I had a hard time thinking up a nickname for. Usually they just come to me. Brown hair, brown eyes, average height. He was like a social chameleon. I could tell he was impatiently waiting for Godhead to introduce us as the other two went down in flames. He complimented the pad a little too vigorously. I mean, it was kind of a dump. I could tell he was thinking of what to say for maximum effect. Salesman mentality.

"Easy there, Tiger," I wanted to say. "You're trying too hard." I decide to call him the Boot Licking Toady after that pathetic display of groveling. Hey, I know it was cruel, but it was the only thing I could come up with spur of the moment style.

I tore off the cap to my beer and tossed it into the sink filled with dirty dishes. The three who took beers had already opened theirs and were desperately searching for a garbage can to throw their caps in. Reluctantly they followed my example. I could tell by the sound only, because I had already turned and padded through the kitchen door, leaving them to take their first meek sips. I got down one good suck as I walked into my room.

Caught a glimpse of the reflection of my naked body in the window as I stripped off the towel and threw it on my bed. God, I was one bony motherfucker: all angles, skin, and a little bit of gristle hanging between my legs. Thin arms, sunken chest, looked like I was starving to death. My clothes hung off me. Always hoped I would fill out but never did anything about it. Like what? Join a gym, become a no-neck, iron pumping, steroid victim? No way. I would rather stay a skinny loudmouth little punk. At least it was a conscious decision.

It was weird, even in the blurry reflection from the window I could make out the quiltwork of scars covering my body. And I do mean covering. Thin white ribbons of scar tissue adorned my arms, legs, hands, back, face, and head. I liked them. Each scar was a reminder of blood and pain, a learning experience.

Most of the larger patches of road rash were from skateboarding. I had a craving for speed. Nothing like the cheese grater action of falling on asphalt at thirty miles per hour. Your knees and elbows bear the brunt of most of the abuse, with your shins being a close third, but I wasn't limited to those areas.

Once, while skating in an empty drainage ditch, I fell and slid through the remnants of a broken bottle on my back with no shirt on. Left some really good scars. Long ropy ones that itched for days.

Hell, I even rode over my own hand once. Tore off the tip of my left ring finger, yanking a bunch of flesh from underneath the nail. Talk about natural ability. Well, at least I could remember where those scars came from. It was the mystery ones that bothered me.

Sometimes I would wake up in the morning with huge claw marks on my face and chest. Long furrowed scratches that usually ran solitary but sometimes in pairs. The fresh wounds in the morning mirror scared me. I was constantly chewing my nails down to the bleeding quick, so how I inflicted these scratches with nothing but hang nails, ragged nubs for fingertips, was beyond me. It got so I was almost afraid to go to sleep.

Probably had something to do with the nightmares. I had been having them for the last couple of years. Every morning the vomit clawing at the back of my throat waking me up. Staring down at my hands as if they didn't belong to me. Trying to remember what happened.

She was always in the nightmares. I could remember her face

snarling in hatred. Clinched fists pummeling my face and body. I never raised my hands to defend myself. Just took my punishment like I had learned to. Her rage increased, curses escaping her straining lips, until I was a bloody pulp at her feet. It was if I was mute, I could never say a word. That's when I would snap awake with a wild-eyed jerk.

Those were the nightmares. They weren't as bad as the dreams. The dreams left me feeling so low, it would take a couple of days to crawl out of the hole. Made me almost wish for the nightmares.

She would walk into my dream looking even more beautiful than I remembered. Unconsciously, I held my breath so as not to ruin the moment. I watched her come towards me. All I wanted was to reach out and hold her. Unasked, she wrapped her arms around me. I could sense the pressure of her embrace against my back. The sweet smell of her hair, right there in my nose. The tension of her body against mine. I actually felt good.

That's when I would wake up. My arms were empty and I would realize she was gone. She was never coming back. I repeated it over and over to make myself believe. I would wrap my arms around myself and squeeze, feeling empty, hoping that I would shatter.

I couldn't bring myself to say her name. I didn't know why, I just couldn't. It brought back too much. The last three years spent mute, unyielding. I only thought of 'Her' or 'She'. There was no one else anyway.

I walked over to my dresser and pulled open the top left hand drawer in search of some underwear. Three frayed pairs laid there forlornly. One old pair of Jockey's. I hated those tidy-whities that kind of lift and separate. I never wore them and definitely didn't need them. I think they were a legacy from the last time my mother bought me underwear. Shit, were they really that old? Jesus, vintage underwear.

My other options were almost as bad. A pin-striped pair of boxers with the crotch blown out and a threadbare plaid pair of boxers. Grim choices. I went for the plaid boxers.

Man, I desperately needed to do laundry. My pile of dirty

clothes dominated the closet, spilling out onto the floor in a twisted heap. I could barely see a pair of black semi-clean Ben Davis's entwined near the top of the mound. I walked over to the pile and picked them out. A blue cotton work shirt, one of the only clean things I had left, hung limply in the closet next to a dozen empty hangers. I walked over to the bed and sat down to begin dressing. As I pulled on the pants I noticed no major stains, good choice. The shirt still smelled flowery, like those cheap fabric softener sheets they sold at the laundromat, and felt good against my skin. I stood up and walked back over to the dresser for socks.

The contents of the top right hand drawer presented me with a dilemma. There weren't any actual matching pairs, just an assortment of sundry socks I had collected over the past couple of years. Every time I did my laundry I inevitably wound up with a brotherless sock. If anyone left the odd clean sock laying around the laundromat I'd take that one home, too. I didn't have the guts to throw them away, so I kept the orphans around for just such an emergency.

Fished around until I came up with a pair that at least resembled each other, about the same length and texture. One was an all white tube sock. The other, an athletic sock with a red stripe bordered by two blue. Found my black lace-up work boots in a corner as I walked back to my bed and sat down. I got my boots on with little trouble but heard the band of the athletic sock begin to rip as I pulled it on.

"That one is on its way out," I made a mental note.

I glanced around frantically for my Saint Christopher medal. It wasn't on the nightstand. I didn't want to lose that thing. I had been wearing it religiously (ha ha) for the last year and a half.

I bought the medal from this little old lady at the Ashby Flea Market. It was pretty ornate with Saint Christopher carrying some baby on one side and Saint George battling a dragon on the other. She told me it was circa World War II.

The story was loving parents gave them to their patriotic sons as they left for combat to insure their return. Saint Christopher was the patron saint of travelers and, I guess, Saint George was the patron saint of going to war, killing shit, or something to that effect. I knew that old Chris had been de-canonized as a saint by the Catholic Church for crimes of misrepresentation. Apparently there never was a Saint Christopher, the whole deal was a fraud, but, I figured anything with that much popular myth behind it must have something on the ball. Besides, call me superstitious but it made me feel somehow a little safer to have it around my neck.

I finished my beer and retraced my footsteps into the bathroom. The Saint Christopher medal twinkled up at me from the sink where I had left it. I slipped the chain over my head. Relief.

Next to it was my watch: a black plastic Casio digital that perfectly matched the untanned band around my wrist. I couldn't live without that watch. It was an auditory thing. The loudest fucking watch I could find. I always had it set in the 'chime' mode. Hours were marked by that grating digital beep. It was so fucking annoying. I loved it. Every hour lost. Beep, beep.

It reminded me that I was slowly dying, wasting time. Hell, it even interrupted conversations. My watch would announce another lost hour and I would trail off mid-sentence, forgetting what I was saying. Looking down at my watch, thinking about my mortality. Knowing that it really didn't matter anyway. What difference could it make?

Sometimes late at night the watch would wake me up. I would lay there and listen to the grains of sand falling in my head. Another heartbeat closer.

There was even a game I would play with that watch. After it notified me of another squandered increment of my life I used to try to see how fast I could look down at the actual time. Two seconds was my personal best, hands free. Three seconds, fists in pockets, and eight out of a deep sleep. Pretty fucking quick if you ask me. I put the Casio on. Outfit complete.

Stared at myself in the bathroom mirror one last time before walking out. Lookin' good: huge bags under red rimmed eyes, three day old razor stubble, fucked-up flat top, broken nose angled ever so slightly to the left, the whole nine yards. I got that broken nose for my seventeenth birthday.

It was September 24, 1981, a Friday night, and I had gone to see Crucifix, the Lewd, and Flipper at the Mabuhay Gardens. Even though it was my birthday, I had been volunteered to drive, being the only one with access to their parents' car. The folks thought I was going to the movies. I lied.

Once again I had the pleasure of staying semi-sober and chauffeuring Stan and his girlfriend Margaret, Jim, and my girlfriend at the time, Debbi, to and from a show. Stan, Jim and I hung tight in high school. I would have done anything for those two and pretty much did. We were Albany High's original punk set. Tough as nails and punker than thou. No values.

I picked everyone up and we cornered a twelve-pack of Mickey's down at Pic-N-Pac Liquors on the corner of Gilman and San Pablo. There were already a couple of regulars hanging out front, so scoring the fine malt liquor was no problem. All it cost was our self-esteem, the change on the beer, and one of the bottles from the twelve-pack. In the parking lot we cracked a Big Mouth and toasted my birthday.

Stan and Margaret had cut school earlier on in the afternoon. They were fucked-up already, having hit the bottle of vodka hidden at Stan's house, so they only got one Mickey's to share between the two of them, not really needing it.

I don't know if it was because I was standing under a sputtering arc light in a deserted parking lot with the wind blowing in my face, but that Mickey's tasted really good. Cold, slightly bitter, and definitely illegal as fuck. Debbi had slipped me a couple of Black Beauties when the rest of them weren't looking, part of my birthday present, and I swallowed them with a gulp of beer after biting the caps. Made for a better rush.

We polished off our respective beers and climbed into the parents' '69 Mercury Cougar and I pointed it towards San Francisco. Another beer was definitely in order. The ride across the Bay Bridge went off without a hitch. Barely any trouble with the toll-guy as I handed him a buck. Unfortunately for Jim, the happy lovin' couple in the back seat with him started making out. Always makes you feel comfortable.

We rolled down the Broadway exit from the Embarcadero Freeway in high spirits. I took the first right, looking for a spot to toss the car in. The Adolescents album was playing on the little battery powered cassette player we brought with us. We all sang along, knowing the words by heart, front to back. I could hear Jim, Stan and Margaret from the back seat, pipe in with the chorus to 'Creatures' as Debbi and I sung the verses. Jim was perfectly out of key and rhythm. Would have made a great singer.

I almost didn't want to turn the engine off but we were already parked. When I saw the parking spot I was tempted to just keep on driving. We sat for awhile with the engine off listening to the end of the album. I felt good, my birthday was going better than expected. Jim handed me one of the last three beers. I pounded mine as they passed around the other two. We finished about the same time. I belched loudly.

Nothing to do now but go to the show. The car doors locked behind us and we walked up around the block to Broadway. Jim, Debbi and I eagerly made our way up the hill towards the Mab skipping, laughing and pushing each other. I looked over my shoulder to check on the other two. They lagged about twenty yards behind. I guessed they needed to share a little special time together. Fucking lovebirds, ain't it cute?

We lost them to some dark alley after a block. Stan and Margaret had a tendency to disappear at the drop of a hat. We paid it no nevermind.

I saw some faces I recognized from the East Bay scene as we came upon the doors to the show. For some reason there seemed to be a larger crowd than usual hanging out front, showing off their latest attire. The fashion show paraded in front of me, participants posturing for maximum effect.

I milled about shooting the shit with people I hadn't seen in awhile. Caught up with Tim Shmeclock out in front of the doors. 'Shmeclock' was one of those drunken nicknames, given while downing quarts, that had stuck. Tim was one of the kinderpunks. Fourteen, shaved head, always amped up, on or about something. The kid was spontaneous human combustion, or at least a really bad accident just waiting to happen.

I hadn't seen Tim hanging out on Telegraph Avenue in a while. Rumor had it he was spending a little time in Juvie for 'Minor In Possession'. Got busted at Willard with a quart of Rainier. Pretty petty, if you ask me. He didn't hear Johnny Puke call out "Six-Up," as the cops rolled by. Everyone else split leaving him holding the bag, literally. They decided to make an example out of him. "What a fucking drag," was all I could say.

I asked Tim about the accommodations. He exploded into a full blown docudrama about the horrors of the California Juvenile Detention System, complete with arrest, booking and gratuitous full body cavity search. The punchline to the whole fucked situation was his mother wouldn't throw his bail. She was gonna let him rot.

"Fucked-up or what?"

Finally the father he hardly ever saw came and got him out.

"The Old Man was pissed."

We stood for a second laughing. It wasn't really funny but we did anyway. I took a deep breath. My scalp prickled with a rush as the Beauties hit home. My vision crystallized, shoving aside the alcohol. I noticed people were hanging out but no one made any actual effort to line up to enter the Mab. Tim caught me staring, eyes bugging out.

"They're cardin' tonight - eighteen and older admitted only," he offered in explanation. "Pigs came by earlier."

"Just my luck," I groaned. "Happy fucking seventeenth birthday."

I had a three way combo going: it was cold, I wasn't getting into the show, and I didn't have my jacket. We had left them in the car because the Mab was like a toaster oven except with less ventilation. Basically, we were rat fucked. I looked around and located Jim in the crowd. He was with Debbi down by the Arcade next to the Mab. They were in some heated discussion with a big hulking skinhead while another one looked one, arms crossed. I could hear the booming voice of the girthy one as he brought his point home, finger in Jim's face.

"Man," I gulped, "the last thing I want is to get in a fight on my birthday."

It was Brent and Sam, I realized with relief. Two guys that used to go to Albany High with us. I say 'used to' because they dropped out soon after 'going punk' (da da-dum dum). Couldn't hang with the flack from the jocks. Brent recognized me walking up out of the corner of his eye. Theatrically, he broke off his tirade and jumped for my throat, getting me in a headlock.

"Happy fucking birthday," Brent screamed, giving a couple of knuckle shots to my skull. He walked me around the sidewalk like a big time wrestler. I was pretty much at his mercy, meaty bicep wrapped around my throat.

Brent was a big kid back we first met in high school. Jim, Sam and him had been friends since middle school, but by then he had almost finished filling out, teenage growth spurt and all. Barrel chest, broad shoulders. Brent liked to show off his new musculature. However, I was still taller than him and I guess it irked his ire. Born with something to prove, don't ask me what. He could kick my skinny little ass in a minute. Finally, I shrugged my way out of his grip, ears burning. Sam eyed me flatly, like a PBS program.

"Happy birthday, man," he said in his best bored voice.

Sam was like that. Cold as ice and cooler than thou. We used to live in the same neighborhood, our parents had known each other for years, and he still played that stranger shit with me. I guess that was just how Sam was. Always seemed kind of distant.

"Thanks, man," I answered calmly, rubbing my ear.

I explained the situation to Debbi and Jim. Gaining entrance to said event looked mighty slim. Out of the three of us, Debbi was the closest to eighteen years of age, being only a couple of months shy. Imagine, I was shacking up with an older woman.

Plan B was in full effect: quarts in the alley between the Mab and the Arcade next door. The only drawback was wind chill factor minus zero. We agreed to cruise back to the ride in search of jackets, Stan and Margaret. We made it as far as two blocks.

I was in the lead, walking down the hill towards the car as they passed. Two Pinole biker redneck types drinking Budweiser out of bottles and looking for a little fun in the big city. I guess they found it. Us.

The bigger of the two easily had two inches and sixty pounds on me, and I was the biggest between me and Jim. Greasy long dirty blonde hair parted straight down the middle, his flecks of dandruff were highlighted by the streetlight. Both wore jean jackets with cut-off sleeves and dark blue corduroy bell bottoms. The shorter one had a brass Led Zeppelin belt buckle. I took this all in with a glance as they passed, the bigger one snarling, "Fucking punkers, I oughta kick your ass."

I let them by without saying shit, I wasn't going to fuck with it. They, however, weren't going out like that. A bottle hissed past my ear and exploded on the sidewalk in front of me. My head involuntarily whipped around. It was treated to a view of the rednecks (for here on out to be known as 'Necks) marching back.

"Fucking punkers, I'm gonna kick your ass," the 'Neck decided to make good on his offer.

I glanced around frantically for a direction to run. Cars presented a solid wall, parked bumper to bumper against the curb. The corner at the end of the block seemed impossibly far away, telescoping off into the distance.

"Oh fuck, oh fuck, oh fuck...," I couldn't help but repeat it to myself like a litany.

Me and Jim were backpedaling down the block as fast as our little feet would carry us, watching the 'Necks come down after us. Debbi fell back against a wall forgotten. The 'Necks had obviously chosen their targets because the bigger one peeled out of formation to confront me.

Out of the corner of my eye I spied an empty champagne bottle lying in the gutter next my feet. I picked it up, hefting the bottle in my hand. I watched Mr. Big 'Neck reach into his back pocket and yank something out. I realized it was a knife as he pulled the blade free of the handle. It caught the light reflecting it clean and sharp. We sized each other up. It was pretty clear I was gonna get my ass kicked.

"Put down the knife," I offered, not wanting to get shanked, "and I'll put down the bottle."

I don't know what the fuck I was thinking.

To my surprise, I heard the blade shut with a snap as he stuffed it back into his pocket. The champagne bottle hit the sidewalk with a clatter. What the fuck was I thinking?

Mr. Big 'Neck circled, looking for an opening. My eyes followed him. Jim came into view. Just in time to see him take a good shot to the gut from the smaller 'Neck. Debbi stood against the wall with a look of horrible fascination as if she wanted to run but was rooted to the spot for the duration of this sordid little scene.

His first shot came soon enough, a kick to the stomach with those big logger boots that were so fashionable at the time with inbred white trash, that I mostly blocked with my forearms. Nonetheless, the force of it knocked most of the wind out of me. I couldn't go down or I was dust. He had left himself open.

I came back with a punch towards the head that was easily deflected. His next kick caught me squarely in the solar plexus, doubling me over. The punch that followed, straight to the side of my head, sent me to my knees. I looked up. A couple of feet over Jim was on all fours holding his side. Through the stars I could see the Mr. Big 'Neck screaming in triumph, "That's right, motherfucker. Stay down!"

I couldn't have gotten up even if I wanted to. The 'Necks ran up the block laughing. The blood pounding in my head was shattered by Debbi's voice. She kept asking if I was alright, over and over again, in a high pitched hysterical voice. It scared me more than what had just happened.

"Yeah, I'm alright," I answered more for my own benefit than hers.

I pulled myself up on wobbly legs, shaking all over. I walked over to help Jim up. He was struggling to stand. I could feel the skin of my face tighten as the cheekbone swelled. Jim fared no better than me, clutching his stomach. We stood there taking a couple of shaky breaths, trying to get our nerve back.

"Jesus Christ," I laughed nervously. "What was that all about?"

We realized it wasn't over yet. Those two could be lurking around anywhere. Or worse, coming back for more.

"What do you wanna do?" I asked Jim.

We decided to try and make it back to the Mab. I wasn't cold anymore, at least I didn't notice if I was. Hopefully, we could blend in with the crowd before the 'Necks located us for round two. We sprinted up the block and made the green light. The Mab was only a half block from there. It took forever, like a bad nightmare, running through water.

After the crowd swallowed us up, I looked over my shoulder to make sure we weren't being followed. Not a 'Neck in sight. We stood there counting our blessings as Brent strolled up.

"What the fuck is wrong with you two?" I guess he noticed. We quickly outlined what happened. Brent couldn't believe it.

"No fucking way," he screamed.

Some of the Berkeley/East Bay scene types had gathered around the commotion to find out what was up. That was when Jim spotted the 'Necks walking across the street. There were four of them now. Four greasy, hulking redneck types.

"Let's get 'em!" I don't remember who said it. We had all been chased, threatened and/or jumped by guys or crowds bigger than any or all of us. It was just one of those things, came with the P-rock territory. You became a target in more ways than one.

However, this time we had superior numbers. Brent took the lead, followed by Sam, Jim and a friend of Sam's named Turner. Me and another guy hung back to the rear of the mob. I looked over at him. "Man, the last thing I want to do is get into a fight. It's my birthday," I added almost in explanation.

"Me neither," was his reply. "I'm kinda drunk."

We introduced ourselves. His name was Erin. I recognized him from Telegraph Ave but didn't know his name.

Our crowd followed the 'Necks on the other side of the street, down Broadway to Columbus. The light changed and we crossed Broadway en masse. The 'Necks had realized we were coming for them and had stopped about a quarter of a block away, gathering their courage. We stood on the sidewalk in front of the Condor, under Carol Doda's blinking neon tits, gathering ours.

Between the six of us, we didn't have many weapons. Brent carried a knife. Said it was for packing his fist. Give his meaty paw some more weight. Make it solid and heavier.

"Yeah, right," was my answer to that.

Sam was wearing a belt made out of chromed motorcycle chains. It was heavy and when swung made a good club. He pulled it from around his waist.

We stood in a circle trying to decide what to do. I'd personally had enough of being punched and trying to punch people. I let them know so.

Maybe this isn't such a good idea, was the general consensus.

We stood in a cluster waiting for the light to cross Broadway again. I had my back to the 'Necks.

"Hey," someone shouted behind me.

I spun around clockwise to look over my shoulder. The first bottle thrown hit me in the side of the head about two inches above my right ear, exploding on contact. Back down to my knees.

I came to with one of the 'Necks standing over me. I didn't recognize him and realized he was one of the two new ones. I grabbed around the knees, trying to tackle him. Bit off more than I could chew.

The 'Neck grabbed me by the head and proceeded to smash my face into the pavement. Repeatedly. I was only conscious for the first smack. I had to hear about the rest of it later on.

Jim watched as my face hit the sidewalk, for as many times as he could stand. He punched the 'Neck as hard as he could in the face. Ordinarily this wouldn't have had much of an effect on the 'Neck, but Jim had the foresight to wrap the bondage bracelet (with rings and a big lock on it) he was wearing, around his little fist. The 'Neck's face opened with a splash, splattering Jim with blood. That 'Neck staggered off holding his ruined face. Jim knelt, trying to shake me awake.

Apparently, the second bottle thrown shattered on Erin's jaw, breaking it. He went down also. The QB of that particular pass, ran up and kicked Erin right in the nuts. Without thinking, Sam lashed out with the chrome chain belt, wrapping it around the 'Neck's head. He hit the ground without even trying to break his fall. Two for two. Sam backed off, realizing what he had done.

Meanwhile, the final bottle went straight for Turner's throat, sending him to the pavement also. A 'Neck jumped on him and began pummeling his face. Brent pulled his knife blade free of its handle and stabbed the 'Neck right in his back. Later, Brent told me he felt it sink in and hit a rib. The knife was torn out of his grasp as the 'Neck twisted underneath him, groaning.

Only two left standing, Brent and my friend from earlier on, Mr. Big 'Neck. He had twenty pounds and a good three or four inches on Brent. But as I said earlier on, Brent was a psycho and had something to prove.

They went toe to toe. Just stood their and traded punches, no finesse necessary. Mr. Big 'Neck was jackhammered to the ground. He looked around in a daze, realizing his buddies were down also. No white trash cavalry. Brent looked around in triumph, the only one left standing.

That was when he saw the rest of us. Jim had turned me over, horrified to find me geysering blood from my head, nose, and face. Turner had started to come to some, barely sitting up. Erin was still laid out like a broken doll, face swelling where the bottle had broken his jaw. I don't know where Sam was. Mr. Big 'Neck had already gathered up his fallen comrades and limped off.

The Condor's barker had already dialed the police, practically having their own hotline. Jim was sure I was dead so he didn't notice the approaching sirens. The police arrived about five minutes later. According to Jim, a stripper wandered out in a red satiny, frilly robe and gave him ice to put on my head. Jim swore he could see her tits.

I came to, in the back of an ambulance, left eye swollen shut. Blood streaming down my face. I looked over and to my surprise, who was sitting next to me nursing a broken face, but Erin. Pretty good for the two guys who didn't want to get in a fight on a Friday night. The ambulance drivers waited around long enough for a cop to take my statement before cutting to the hospital. I tried to explain what happened but before I could really get into it, the cop's partner interrupted me.

"Don't bother," he stated in an annoyed voice. "It's always their fault."

The cop shut his logbook and mind with a snap, and instructed the driver to move along.

I had to call my mother from the pay phone in the hospital Emergency Waiting Room to come sign the consent forms so a doctor could sew up my head. It was about midnight. I sat waiting for her to show up.

In the hour it took her to get there, a couple of people from the Mab showed up. Somehow, Debbi had ended up with my keys and after finding Stan and Margaret, gave them all a ride over to the hospital, including Brent. Someone, I don't remember who, passed me a half-empty bottle of vodka. I threw as much as I could stomach down my sticky, rust flavored throat. I mumbled something about a fucked up birthday, and the waiting room full of punks broke into an off-key rendition of 'Happy Birthday To You'.

The irony of it made me grin, the pain twisting the smile off my face as soon as it began to flower. My nose finally stopped bleeding a few minutes before the Old Lady showed up. It had been going for like an hour. I knew it was broken. Not to the side, but crushed straight down into my face so it didn't look too bad yet, just beginning to really swell.

My mother made her appearance, signed the necessary forms, and in we went to see the good doctor. Oh happy day, medical attention.

He took one look at my head and shaved out a four inch patch above my right ear, exposing the ragged gash made by the Budweiser bottle breaking against my skull.

"It'll make you look punk." Doc thought he was funny. He astutely observed that I was already anesthetized and proceeded to sew up my scalp without the benefit of a local. I could feel the bite and pull of each stitch. After what seemed an eternity of this, the pain finally stopped. My head was relatively back in one piece. I asked him about the broken nose.

"Your nose isn't broken, tough guy," he said, giving me one of those light slaps to the face meant to convey I was alright or something, "or it would still be bleeding."

The dull pain in my head exploded with a flash, bringing tears to my eyes. Fuck, the last thing I wanted at that point was for this guy to set my nose. Probably enjoy it too much. I'd had enough of that bullshit. I pulled myself up off the table, blinking at the throbbing in my head.

"Thanks a lot, dude," I said, trying to act cavalier, just to piss him off.

My nose was definitely broken. The next day it was all swollen up, black circles under my eyes. I never got it set. It healed with a slight hook to the left, the right nostril closing down so I found it hard to breathe out of that side. Too late to do anything about that now, I thought as I exited the bathroom.

The idiots had gone back to watching MTV I realized, as I rounded the corner to the living room. To Godhead's credit, he was absentmindedly thumbing through a stack of old magazines piled on the coffee table. I guess MTV didn't do it for him either. I noticed they weren't even halfway done with their beers yet, as I stood there. The timid pocket mice seemed anxious about making this party on time because they were no longer mesmerized by the images of scantily clad nubiles frolicking in MTV-land. The Boot Licking Toady and Curly both looked over at Gary as if on cue but Radar just stared off into the TV screen.

"Ready to go?" asked Godhead, the obvious mouthpiece for the group. The rest of them didn't have the juice to speak up.

"I'm gonna get me another beer," I stated as I walked out of the room. "Finish yours up."

I left them in living room to bounce their worried looks off each other. Like they were going to miss something showing up late to this little soiree. Fuck 'em, they need a little tension in their lives, it might do them some good, I thought, put an edge on the evening. Give something for their anxious little minds to really stew on.

The kitchen was dark but I didn't turn on the light. The bulb in the fridge glowed golden as I yanked open the door. Two beers left out of the six-pack so I grabbed one and shoved the other back behind a milk carton for future reference. My motherfucking roommates had a tendency to drink my last beer if I didn't camouflage it behind some expired dairy product or moldering head of lettuce.

The worst part of the whole situation was, if I confronted them about it, one would look at me innocently and invariably say something to the effect of, "Oh, I thought someone was being cool and left me a beer for after work. Sorry, man, I'll pay you back."

I always ended up feeling like one of the lowest miserly assholes that has ever crawled the earth. However, I never did see any of that beer.

I twisted off the cap and flicked it into the sink. I could smell the dishes in the sink, starting to take on a life of their own. The pale darkness was kind of comforting, so I sat down at the kitchen table for my first sip. It was good to have a minute to myself before going out. I just sat there thinking about nothing. My time alone was important to me, especially when faced with an evening of amateur drinkers. A little alcohol courage and they think they're on top of the world. It was pathetic to see someone you don't even know, get all bent up and make a fool of themselves. Leave it to the professionals. I stood up in the gray twilight of the kitchen, drained my beer, and set it on the counter next to the stacked sink.

"I'm as ready as I'll ever be," the words echoed off the linoleum floor. I looked at my dim reflection in the kitchen window and grinned sheepishly. Why the fuck do I do this shit to myself?

Walked back into the living room. They had finished their beers by now, I noticed. Three empty soldiers stood at attention in a cluster at one end of the coffee table. MTV was still on but the sound was turned way down so the commercials were unintelligible mumbling.

"Let's cut out," I couldn't help but use the vernacular, hoping to confuse them.

They stood, voicing their agreement as I switched off the TV with the remote. Godhead let them out as I turned off the lights in the living room and grabbed my jean jacket. Checked my pockets for keys, wallet and money, all in that order, as I shut the door. The mob was about half a landing ahead of me on the stairs but I caught up to them before the last step. The wrought iron gate/front door slammed shut behind us with a crash. We were t-rolling over to the party in Curly's fine chariot. The '82 Volkswagen Scirocco was parked about a half a block up in front of a fire hydrant. That explains the wild hair up their asses to get this show on the road, I thought as I climbed into the back seat, sandwiched between Radar and the Boot Licking Toady. I hated riding bitch, the hump always made my bony butt ache, but didn't say anything. It was only as far as the Sunset from the Fillmore. The party was out in the Ave's.

We drove most of the way in silence except for the occasional "Goddammit!" from Curly. I wasn't ready to run the gauntlet. He, on the other hand, was all over the road. We jockeyed for pole position in the crosstown evening traffic. Taxis, pedestrians, red lights, the instinct to survive - nothing was going to slow him down. Unfortunately, from my seat, I had the best view of the action in the house. Several were the times I was witness to a frantically spinning steering wheel, squealing tires and some quick heel-toe action. Somehow I kept my mouth shut through it all, but there were several close calls. I vowed to get a seatbelt on the way back, or die trying.

We went screaming by one of my favorite landmarks in the Sunset on the way. Shit, I liked the look of the place and I had never been inside. Just one of those joints that made my head turn. Anytime I passed by on the N-Judah I promised myself to go inside and order a beer someday, but nothing ever really brought me to the neighborhood.

I was always just passing by, but never stopping. I guess it was significant only to me but The Embers looked like a cool place to hunker down in. A bar where no one bothered you. You could drink and think in peace, two activities that don't usually lend well to each other, except in certain dingy bars.

We found parking on the street, right next to the party. The house was on Funston below Judah. One of those stucco jobs painted beige with dark brown trim. I hated that gingerbread house look.

There was no 13th Ave for some inane reason. The streets went 12th, Funston, 14th. Fuck bad luck. I thought it would be dope to have an address on 13th, spooky as hell.

I didn't hear anything unusual, as we piled out of the car, that would betray a party in progress. No shooting, shouting or breaking glass. Just the traffic sliding by on Judah and the hum of the electric street lights.

"Must be really happening," I teased sarcastically.

I was just funnin' with them. The timid pocket mice looked at me puzzled, not getting the joke. I ignored them. As we walked up the front steps, Godhead in the lead as usual and me lagging a few steps behind, I began to hear the soft strains of bad 'Modern Rock'. Sounded like an old Wang-Chung record was playing.

"Couldn't be," my mind reeled. "Where the fuck did they dig that up from?"

Gary rang the bell and not five seconds later the door was yanked open by a bleached blonde with big sprayed-up bangs. That was all I could see over their shoulders. Her hair eclipsed the doorway. She had to have been standing right next to the front door, waiting to greet people. There was no other way Blondie could have answered the door that quickly. Must be our hostess, I guessed.

"Gary, you're late," she whined disapprovingly, confirming my theory.

She moved out of our way to let us file in or cigarette smoke billow out, I wasn't sure which. Godhead introduced me to The Hostess as I stepped into the cloud, but I didn't catch her name because A-Ha broke into their one and only hit. We shook hands briefly and she shut the door. I stood there awkwardly, cut off from my only escape route.

Godhead and the rest had wandered off to greet different cliques of people standing around the room. It was a large room, more like a combo living/dining room. Big enough for a dining roomesque table and chairs back by the far wall. A stereo rack leaned up against the fireplace. The couch, easy chair and coffee table ensemble was situated to form a separate living room area. They cowered in front of the TV set, up near the front windows. The Hostess made no motion to walk away from the door. She scrutinized me carefully as I eyeballed the crowd.

"Soooo..." she asked, drawing out the 'o' in a condescending voice, "how do you know Gary?"

"I used to drink a lot with Godhead in college," I tried to sum it up the best I could, not looking at her.

The crowd was pretty tame, if you asked me. About eight average-looking white guys and three of their chicks stood talking in small groups. A set of four of these guys and a girl were crowded around the dining room table. It was littered with tortilla chip crumbs, empty salsa bowls, a couple of wilted celery sticks, some vegetable dip and the odd crust of French bread. They just stood there idly picking at the remains of the buffet table. Too late for any serious snacking.

A guy and his girlfriend sat on the couch with beers in their hands, talking in low voices. The other three dudes in the front room had cornered the remaining free girl over near the stereo. They were vigorously pumping her for information. She looked like she was enjoying their attention, don't ask me why. Can't she tell what hard-up dorks they are? The question seemed obvious to me.

I could see into the kitchen where another clique was in a heated discussion. A couple of the guys were giving me the once over but I didn't detect any hostility yet, just curiosity.

I don't know what it was about the way I held my face, dressed, made eye contact or whatever, but I attracted trouble like moths to a flame. For some unknown reason, the biggest, most belligerent drunk always seemed to single me out for a li'l one on one. Never a dull moment.

"Oh well," I breathed a sigh of relief. "Safe for the time being."

The Hostess must have decided I was all right because I heard, "The keg is out in the kitchen," from her direction.

I thanked her and began to make my way across the living room. To my left was a doorway that opened into a small hall which must have led to the bathroom and master bedroom. I continued on into the kitchen.

Gary was bullshitting with some tall blonde guy in a white buttondown shirt. I noticed Godhead already held a plastic keg cup in his hand and was sidling on up to the tap. I had lost track of Radar, Curly and the Boot Licking Toady to my relief. Gary waved me over as I stepped into the kitchen.

Damn, he had good manners, because once again I found myself being introduced to someone whose name I immediately forgot. Ted or Tom or something. We shook hands briefly but I broke it off early because I was sick of all these pointless rituals.

I remembered when I was a little kid, I promised myself never to shake hands with people. I didn't know what it was, but shaking hands seemed like something phony adults did when greeting someone they would rather punch in the face. I could still see it in their eyes. They just weren't up front about it. You could always tell when another kid didn't like you. No candy coated message.

Anyway, this didn't fly well with my newfound friend. His eyes narrowed suspiciously and he took a deep breath, puffing out his chest. I stared back coldly. There was a moment of tension. A little open confrontation would have been a welcome change. I wanted to tell him to bring on the weak shit. Godhead broke the silence, shoving a cup in my hand. "Pump that thing, man."

I reached down and gave the tap a couple of absentminded pumps. Gary and Tense-Guy went back to their conversation. I could tell Tense-Guy was watching me out of the corner of his eye. They were having one of those pointless 'talking shop' sort of gripe sessions. Bitching about the work heaped on them by the higher-ups. Waste of breath. I mean, that's what management was for, wasn't it obvious? Must be one of Godhead's co-workers, I decided.

I looked around the kitchen and out into the living room. Cliques of unfamiliar people posturing in idle conversation. Made me feel far away, like a voyeur. The actual distances between people seemed like miles. The Hostess still manned her position over by the front door. She seemed like the perfect target. Not only was no one talking to her, but it was her party so she had to be polite. I thought it might be a good time to strike up a conversation. The doorbell rang before I could take two steps. I stopped cold in the kitchen doorway.

They made their entrance in grand style, fashionably late. All heads turned and the buzz of conversation ground to a halt. I heard a few people murmur his name, in awe of Prince Late-Guy. He primped in the doorway while The Hostess made a big deal, thanking him for coming and generally drooling all over him. Looked like a jerk with a capitol 'J' to me.

Black slacks, black turtleneck sweater, black wool sport jacket. Black must have been written up as the new 'in' color in the most recent *GQ* magazine. Sophisticated horn-rimmed glasses. Balding. What was left of his thinning curly brown hair was slicked back in a tight ponytail. Was the mustache and beard some sort of subconscious compensation for his receding hairline, or just the surefire sign of a pompous asshole?

He reached back and swept his woman in out of the cold with a flourish. The whole thing was so staged that it made me sick to my stomach. Like the Queen of England, she played it big, scanning the room with a glance as though it were full of adoring subjects. I don't know if it was the faded blue jeans torn in all the right places, or the bolero style hat perched on top of her Dorothy Hamill gone punk, bleached blonde hairdo that bugged me so fucking much. Black leather jacket, bustier, black pointy shoes. I thought she watched too much Club MTV. She gripped his arm adoringly.

The Hostess's compliments were deflected with a condescending "Thank you."

Served her right, I thought. They sauntered across the floor, greeting the little people like royalty. I watched them work their way back towards the kitchen. I ate up every step. Used it to fuel my anger. By the time they stopped at the doorway I was blocking, I could feel the waves of hostility bristling off me. I was seething. The tingle of an adrenaline rush brought blood to my cheeks. Prince Late-Guy gave me the once over like I was dirt and I returned it just to piss him off. I was looking forward to the altercation, an exchange of insults, anything to get things out in the open, but white folks are the politest people in the world. Sickeningly so.

"Excuse me," he stated, forehead creasing in suppressed frustration.

I hesitated for a second, just to irk his ire, then pushed off the doorjamb, unclogging the doorway. Walked over to the hallway leading off the living room, in search of the bathroom. Ten points. My guess was correct because the toilet was a few feet down, door open. I shut it behind me, unzipping my pants. It took me a second to start pissing, being in unfamiliar facilities. I glanced around haphazardly. Typical girl paraphernalia cluttered the shelves: nail polish remover, baby powder, Q-tips. I could see a small basket full of flower potpourri on the windowsill. The three beers I'd had earlier ran out of me bringing the water in the bowl to a boil. My clear stream whipped a frothy head.

"Man, fuck those two," I was talking out loud. "Who do they think they are?"

I couldn't believe that fucking entrance. Like a debutante at her coming out or a prom date, all flash and flaunt. That kind of egotistical pageantry made me sick. Were we supposed to be envious of their grand lives? All I wanted to do was take them down a notch. I yanked up my pants thinking about that stupid bleach blonde bob haircut.

She stood right outside of the bathroom as I turned off the lights, walking out. Her bolero hat was pushed back off her head, hanging around her neck by the strap. Too much eye makeup. I was surprised - where did Prince Late-Guy go? I mean, they looked inseparable.

"Hi there," she said, just as startled as I was. The sound of her voice tore me out of my shock.

"Hey," I answered gruffly, shouldering my way past her.

I heard the light go on and the door close as I walked down the hall. Shit, there I was standing in the dining room surrounded by people I didn't know, again. The air had taken on a blue tint and burned in my lungs. I hated the way people stood clutching their cigarettes. Exhaling the smoke above my head, as if it helped. Just blow your fucking smoke right into my face, it's practically the same thing.

The keg was unattended. I could see into the kitchen and my cup was empty. Lattice of coincidence? I don't think so. I was filling my cup in no time.

Pretty cool, I thought, peering around. Only had to say four sentences since I got here. I felt good. Didn't have anything to say anyway. I had almost forgotten how to talk to people. Conversations seemed petty and remote, not really having much to do with me. I gave my responses automatically, as if I knew what was expected of me but performed it grudgingly. What I meant was this: what would I have to say to someone else that I couldn't tell myself?

I shuffled out into the living room, cup in hand, looking for something to catch my attention. Anything. The dining room table looked like a battlefield and anything edible had been on the losing side. I stood looking down at the carnage, trying to divine something in the mess. Maybe it could give me some clue to this party I was missing. Nothing came to me. I was just staring at a ravaged deli tray.

"Not much left," someone astutely observed over my shoulder.

Their breath on the back of my neck gave me goosebumps. I cringed slightly in annoyance, looking over my shoulder. It was Little Miss Fashionably-Late. She had to speak loud over the music

"Not much left," she repeated.

Now I was pissed off. What the fuck did she want? Was she trying to push my buttons? I couldn't tell. I was nobody so she was barking up the wrong tree. I stared back at her, shocked that out of all her admirers, she had to fuck with me. Couldn't she tell I wanted to be left alone?

"Who do you know here?" she went on nevertheless, motioning to the rest of the party with her head.

"I don't know anybody," I answered loud enough to be heard over the strains of the tail end of Adam Ant's last hit.

Unfortunately, the tape that was playing outdated New Wave ended with a fat 'click'. It was one of those moments in a lame party where everything grinds to a halt (EF Hutton style) so my statement echoed in the quiet. Heads turned to scrutinize the outsider, I noticed out of the corner of my eye. Fuck. Unconsciously, I blushed.

The timid pocket mice just stood there, looking at me dumbfounded. Probably didn't believe that someone had the nerve to go to a party where he didn't belong. Boy, were they wrong.

I took the two steps necessary to carry me over to the stereo, leaving Li'l Miss Fashionably-Late to flounder on her own. Found the eject button on the tape player. The tape inside popped out with a satisfying 'ka-chunk'. Party Tape '87 was written on the cassette in big, loopy, girl handwriting. It made me laugh. Those songs were already a couple of years out of date by 1987.

I glanced at the pile of tapes on top of the stereo but nothing caught my eye, so I switched the receiver on and spun the dial down into the low end of FM. I was looking for KPOO. They had this cool Funk/Hip-Hop show on Saturday nights. I found it right near 89, on the first pass. Retro-city. Cool. Morris Day and the Time's first hit, was playing.

I heard someone say "Yeah," and a couple people got up to dance. I turned back to the pile of tapes and began rummaging through them for something decent. My mind was made up for me before I could come to a decision.

"What the hell do you think you're doing?" It was the Tense-Guy that Godhead had been griping with earlier. Must be my gracious host. I ignored his question.

I could see a couple of his friends peering out from the kitchen. They had probably run in to tell him that The-Weird-Guy-No-One-Knew was fucking with the stereo. I could tell he was pissed: red-faced, arms folded across his chest. My only way to smooth things over was to apologize profusely for putting the radio on.

"Look, dude, no one was listening to that bullshit." There I went again. The shit just slipped out of my mouth but at least I said it with a smile.

I could tell he was offended by being called "dude." Probably used to being called "Mr." I almost laughed right in his face. I mean, it seemed funny to me. He didn't know what to do. It was his move. We stood there lamely eyeing each other. Li'l Miss Fashionably-Late was watching the whole thing with a look of amusement on her superior face. I was glad someone was enjoying the fireworks.

"Don't fuck with the stereo," Tense-Guy ordered over his shoulder as he walked back over to his pals.

It seemed like a challenge to me. I was tempted to spin the dial just to test his mettle. See him stop dead in his tracks. I mean, guys like that weren't shit until they had a little back-up (strength in numbers and all) but the hassle just didn't seem worth it.

Godhead was over by the front door, talking with The Hostess. Gary didn't seem to want to be associated with me because he didn't make eye contact as I looked over. I could dig it after the scene that had just went down. It was all right, I'd had enough already anyway.

I walked over to where they were standing. Gary looked up in surprise as if it was the first time he had seen me all night.

"Hey," he began uncomfortably. "What's up?"

"I'm gonna cut out," I explained. "I'll be down at The Embers, on Irving, if you wanna get a drink."

It was pointless. Gary wouldn't show up but it was my way of letting him off the hook. Looked like I was gonna get that solitary drink down at The Embers after all.

The Hostess ignored me, peering around at everybody except me, who was standing right in front of her. The message was loud and clear. I had nothing else to say, so I reached out and pulled open the front door.

"That's right. You'd better leave," I heard Tense-Guy say, just loud enough for his friends to hear what a tough guy he was, but low enough so he didn't think I'd hear, as I left.

I stopped in the doorway, looking over my shoulder and slowly turned around. Tense-Guy stood there embarrassed that I'd heard him. He didn't have the juice to come with it. I gave a little laugh because they all looked so stupid standing there. Tense-Guy dropped his eyes to the carpet. I shut the door and was treated to a couple of muffled insults shouted out after they knew I was gone. Tough guys.

I walked down the steps laughing at myself. How the fuck does this kind of bullshit happen to me all the time? I wanted to know. I mean, I went to these kind of gatherings with the best of intentions. Things just tended to get out of hand.

My feet automatically carried me down Funston and right on Irving, towards The Embers. I was there before I knew it.

I stood in front of the door for a second, hesitating, wondering if I should go inside. The Embers. The sign slowly blinked above my head. Looked like a cool neighborhood dive. Dark facade, no windows, and that flashing blue and red neon martini glass.

I pulled open the padded front door. It was dim inside but my eyes adjusted quickly to the dark, having just come in from the night street. The jukebox was about halfway through playing 'What's Goin' On' by Marvin Gaye. There wasn't much goin' on. Two old men sat at the far end of the bar, peering up at a TV set bolted to the wall, heads craned back. The power was on but the sound turned off so it flickered silently above them. I could clearly see their wrinkled throats and sagging chins through the open collars of their shirts. My neck ached from just looking at their position but God knows how long they had been rooted that way.

A plump, middle-aged, matronly woman perched on a stool about halfway down stared at her reflection in the mirror behind the bar. One withered hand was wrapped around a glass of brown liquor over ice and the other clutched the frayed purse in her lap. A sad, down on their luck looking couple sat at a table in the back staring down into their drinks and not saying anything.

The only head that turned to see who it was as I stepped in was the bartender's. I was impressed. The regulars didn't even bother to look up. They were too involved with their own problems to give a fuck about anyone else's. Complete vacuum. Had their own shit to deal with. I was nothing to them, not even worth a glance. Absolute indifference like that was hard to come by. I was jealous, I wished I had the attitude. I like it. I could feel comfortable here.

The bartender stood at the sink about two-thirds of the way down the bar, between the old men and the middle-aged woman. He was leaning back, next to the rack of peanuts, chips and other salted thirst-inducing snacks, washing out some glasses. White apron tied around a thick gut. His face had the lumpy wrinkled look of a boxer or an Irish Catholic priest. Regulars must have called him Rusty or Red or something like that once, but his hair now was mostly gray. He gave me a quick visual inspection. I stepped up to the bar and began to fish for some money in my pockets.

Rusty called out, "Can I help you?" as he came down the bar.

"Can I have a Rolling Rock, please?' I asked. Couldn't hurt to be polite to a new bartender.

"Can-I-see-some-ID?" His syllables slurred together into one long word from years of practice.

I fumbled in my back pocket and yanked out my wallet as Rusty stood staring at me, arms crossed. My driver's license was on top so I slipped that out and handed it over. He stared down at my tattered ID for what seemed an eternity, then suddenly looked up into my eyes as he flipped it onto the bar. Probably thought I looked too young to be twenty-seven, but that was obviously his fucking problem.

"Rolling Rock," he repeated my request.

Rusty turned around without saying another word, leaned over and began rummaging around in a refrigerator under the cash register. I found a twenty dollar bill in my front pocket and smoothed it out on the bar as I took a seat on one of the stools. They were pretty comfortable but the rail under the bar was kind of high, my knees pressed up against the underside of the counter. Wonder what's growing under there, I couldn't help but think.

I turned to look down the bar and noticed the middle-aged lady was no longer staring at her reflection but at me now. There were lines on her forehead and around her mouth like she'd spent a lifetime frowning. Probably thought I looked like a fish out of water. She looked kind of sad so I gave her a little smile. Middle-Aged-Lady returned it with a look of blank indifference, just a vacant stare. I guess she thought I was smirking at her. The smile slipped off my face in pieces.

"That'll be two bucks." Rusty saved me. I turned back feeling stupid. He set my beer down on a napkin and scooped the Jackson off the bar. Man, that beer looked good. Talk about icy fresh - it had already broken out in a cold sweat. One bead of condensation began its long slow slide down the side of the green bottle. I could smell the unmistakable scent of malt and hops as I hefted it to my lips.

The first swallow burned my throat but tasted good, kind of skunky and definitely carbonated. I took two more long sucks and set the bottle down. Rusty came back and threw my change in front of me. I let the bills fall where they may and stared down into this little glass candle holder on the bar. Inside of it was one of those short squat white candles that seem to burn forever with a small yellow flame. My mind began to wander. I started thinking about the walk over from the party.

It happened again on the way. Been awhile since I'd felt like that, but when you least expect it...

I was walking behind a couple, arm in arm. They were strolling along a few yards ahead of me, talking and laughing. He was telling some humorous little anecdote. That lonely/disgusted/angry feeling was coming on fast and furious as they stepped into the light of a street lamp.

"Jesus Christ, I can't believe it," I almost said. My stomach fell and hit bottom with a splash. I felt like throwing up.

There She was. I hadn't seen her in three years but there She was. Beautiful in a feral sense, almost predatory. Long dark hair combed straight back. Black eyebrows arching until they almost met above intense dark eyes. She had a fierce look, severe, for lack of a better word. That sassy walk, like a dancer. Treading on the balls of her feet. Poised, graceful. The way She held his arm. Hand covering her mouth when She laughed, eyes flashing. It was Her. I knew it without having to see her face, just from the body language.

I had to see who She was with. My dull brown eyes bored into his back. I increased my pace to get a good look at his face. Brown leather bomber jacket, black wool sweater, perfectly faded and laundered 501s. His long blonde hair was pulled back in a ponytail. Sophisticated glasses. Not much else. No character to his face, soft around the cheeks, dull. God, I hated those alternative/hip kind of guys. Conceited, confident, walking along like he owned the sidewalk. A politically correct, style conscious, educated type. Looked like he'd never worked a day in his life. Born on the right side of the tracks.

He was everything I hated, I was nothing compared to him. In fact, I was just the opposite. A loser. Why someone like that? The scream echoed in my empty head. I walked along behind them, killing myself. She was happy. I was nothing.

They slowed at the corner, waiting for the green light to cross 10th, as I stumbled upon them. She finally turned enough so I could see Her face.

I realized it wasn't Her. She looked similar but something was missing. That spark, the way she held her face. Something but I wasn't sure what. This particular girl had a soft, boring look. Her neck was thinner, eyes set closer together, different. My stomach fell even further.

It wasn't Her. But that still didn't make it any easier. In fact, it made me feel even worse. I was going to spend my life with the memories, and I had to learn to live with them. Or die with them.

She was gone. That was the long and short of it, no ifs, ands, or buts. I didn't know where She was or who She was with. It had been three years since we'd spoken. I couldn't blame her for never wanting to see me again. I wouldn't know what to say to her anyway.

Thought about it so many times I had gotten lost. The last three fucking years and I was still running the same circles, like a rat in a maze. It was pathetic. I had gone over it time and time again, without getting any closer. What I did and didn't do, what I meant to do, everything.

I couldn't lie if someone asked about her. She deserved better than that. I had to look whoever in the eye and tell them that I cheated on her and She was gone. I couldn't do anything else. Frankly, my friends were fucking sick of it. They told me to get over her. "Forget about it."

How could I do that? If I just forgave and forgot I would never learn anything out of all that happened. I would be doomed to making the same mistake over and over. As if that wasn't my fate already. Was I really any different?

Slowly I realized I should have never said a word to anyone. My mouth clamped shut and I taught myself to isolate. Just work it out in my head. It was a hard lesson to learn.

I had nights standing there, razorblade in my hand. Staring at my wrists, looking for a place to start. Side to side or wrist to elbow? Shit, it was obvious I was trying to kill myself but didn't have the guts. The self-destructive voice inside my head dared me to do it. "Go ahead, you pussy," it snarled. "You don't have the juice."

I hated that voice because it was right.

"I thought so, you fucking coward."

Anyway, the worst part was this: it was all pointless. She would never know, much less care. She was gone. Period. No maybes. I was past the point of suicidal tendencies. I wished I was alive. There wasn't much left anyway.

I couldn't understand it. How could I have done everything I did, to someone that I supposedly cared for? I failed her and myself. Maybe it meant I was a conceited bastard toying with people's emotions like that, but hell, I didn't even really like myself. I took everything I ever believed about Love, Trust and Honor, and smashed it. What kind of human being would do that to another? Obviously not much of one. I was worse than any fucking hypocrite. I was nothing. It was my sentence and I knew it. I took another swallow of beer and glared at the bottle in my hand.

Alcohol wasn't much help. As much as I wished it would, drinking didn't take the edge off. Sharpened it, if anything. The loneliness was a jagged blade I cut myself with constantly. Like doing penance. The pain reminded me I was alive. It was worse to feel nothing at all.

I was miserable and had no one to blame but myself. My free hand was knotted in a fist. I was unconsciously flexing it tighter. Nonexistent nails bit into my palms. I examined my reflection in the mirror behind the bar. It was hard making eye contact. I couldn't fool myself anymore. I knew what I was.

"I hate you," I spat at myself through grinding teeth. I had this crazy urge to hurl my bottle right into that fucking face staring back at me. The mirror would explode with a satisfying smash, but unfortunately I would still be the same. You can run but you can't hide.

She was better off without me anyway. I was poison, the kiss of death. I mean, look what I did to her and myself. It was best to cut your losses while you could. What did I need to prove to myself?

I sat there hammering these thoughts like nails into my skull as I stared down into that little red candle holder. Its flickering glow dominated my field of vision. The blaze caught in the dry tinder of my head. Fire rushed through my veins. Blood like high octane fuel, making my heart race, engines throbbing. I had become the wick to the candle burning beneath me. It seemed so vivid, I could imagine it as clear as day.

The flame consumed my tiny body, hair charring and smoking, fists clenching. My skin began to blister and blacken. I could almost see the body writhing in agony, muscles convulsing. My face had bubbled and begun to run. The ruined mouth opened in a soundless scream. A howl was torn away from my cremated lips. My hands and feet were formless stumps. The smoldering carcass shuddered and slumped forward. My thoughts sank into the blackness. A chill running up my spine snapped me out of it.

My beer was empty. I looked up to catch Rusty's attention. He was down at the sink washing out glasses again but his head turned. I motioned with my bottle, subtly indicating my need for another Rolling Rock. As Rusty bent over to rummage around through the refrigerator under the counter, I heard the front door open.

"Jesus Christ," I moaned in disappointment. Before I could stop it, my head swung around to see who it was. I was gonna have to work on that.

She stood just inside the doorway with a look on her face as if it meant something, her showing up like that. I guess it did. To her. I wondered what happened to the bolero hat. It was Li'l Miss Fashionably-Late from the party. Shit, I had no idea what her name was. I wracked my brain for one, dumbfounded.

"That'll be two bucks," Rusty murmured, setting my beer down on the bar behind me. I could tell he was checking out Li'l Miss Fashionably-Late also from the sound of his voice, so I ignored him.

"I knew you'd be here," she stated, stepping in.

How the hell am I supposed to answer something like that? I was sorely tempted to turn around and ignore her. Hunker down with the locals. Just go back to my drinking and get really fucked up.

She sat down on the empty stool next to me. No escape. I asked her if she wanted a drink, to be polite. Rusty gave me a 'Hey, that's my job' sort of look.

"Cape Cod," she tossed Rusty her order without even bothering to look at him. Man, she sure is used to service. Probably born into money.

"Hey, so... uh...," I didn't know where to start.

"I knew you would be here," Li'l Miss Fashionably-Late repeated as if to clarify herself.

That isn't what I meant, I almost said. More along the lines of: where is your boyfriend? I was having visions of Prince Late-Guy storming in and trying to start some shit. Hell, I was actually looking forward to it. Maybe this night didn't have to end on a sour note after all.

Rusty saved me again by bringing her the drink. I was gonna have to tip him a good one. He gathered the necessary bills off the counter and retreated to the sink. I sat sucking quietly at my beer. Li'l Miss Fashionably-Late sipped her Cape Cod.

"Strong," she exhaled with a grimace.

How the fuck can a Cape Cod be strong, was my unasked question. It's vodka watered down with cranberry juice. I almost laughed in her face, reminding myself to be polite at the last possible moment. Rusty probably made it that way for her special. He stared down the bar, smiling in approval.

Li'l Miss Fashionably-Late was preoccupied with doing what pretty much everyone in the joint, including me, was doing: looking at their reflection in the mirror behind the bar. A half-empty bottle of Wild Turkey obscured my view so I couldn't see the expression on her face. I decide she was reconsidering the wisdom of following me to this dive. She threw back a slug of her drink. I watched her swallow. No Adam's apple.

"What's your name?" I asked. "I never caught your name."

"Katherine," she introduced herself, smiling. Perfect. Not Kathy or Katy, but Katherine. Katherine the Great. I liked it better calling her Li'l Miss Fashionably-Late.

"I'm...," I began, holding my hand out to her because I didn't know what else to do.

"Kurt," she finished for me, shaking my hand.

Now I really was surprised. How the hell did she know my name? We hadn't been introduced and I cut out from the party not long after her and Prince Late-Guy showed up.

I sighted down the neck of the bottle into my beer. It was about half-empty already and getting warm fast. We just sat for awhile saying nothing. I could tell she was looking at me but I concentrated on the beer in front of me.

"I always wanted to come down here." I regretted my statement as fast as it came out of my mouth. Sounded stupid. Like, if that were one of my goals in life, I was pretty pathetic.

The beer I was drinking hadn't been as cold as the first one, I realized. I vowed to finish it off as soon as I could. Finish it off and pack it in. I wanted to go home and be alone again. I went back to staring into the mirror behind the bar. What the fuck do I have to say?

I downed the remainder of the bottle and set it on the bar. Katherine poked her swizzle stick around in the ice cubes of her nearly empty glass and reluctantly followed suit. Rusty mysteriously appeared and asked if we wanted anything else, all smiles. I looked over at Katherine, trying to figure out a way to cut loose the dead weight. She motioned with her empty glass for another Cape Cod before I could pry my mouth open.

"Can I please have another Rolling Rock?" I asked trying to contradict Katherine by being as polite as I could. "And a buck in change."

I think her style worked better than mine because her drink showed up first. Nothing else in Rusty's hands. She fumbled in her jacket while he retrieved my beer.

"Let me get this," Katherine ordered, handing Rusty a ten.

He came back with the change and politely set it before her. Katherine didn't seem to notice, just gathered up her bills, making no motion to tip Rusty. He stood there frowning. We watched her tuck the bills back into her jacket pocket.

"Can I get a buck in change?" I asked again to break the tension.

Rusty's brow wrinkled in frustration but he didn't say anything. Just grabbed one of my dollar bills still lying on the bar and marched off to the cash register. He stomped back and slapped the quarters down in front of me. I gathered up the quarters and remaining bills, all except two dollars, and turned to Katherine.

"I'm gonna put some money into the jukebox." It was more a statement than a question. Katherine must have understood what I meant because she followed me over to the jukebox. I studied the selections, ignoring her. It was hard to, because she was standing close, right next to me. I could hear her breathing. Her perfume was right there, almost overpowering.

Good choices. There were all kinds of oldies, R&B, some soul, and fortunately, no new stuff. The Top 40 shit they loaded those things down with were the worst. I jammed the quarters in the slot and punched E-261. 'Back Stabbers' by The O'Jays. Perfect.

I continued to stare down at the numbers in the jukebox as if trying to decide on another selection. Randomly punched a couple of numbers. I was really wondering what the fuck she was doing there and why the fuck didn't she leave me alone. Finally I couldn't act like I was considering my options anymore. I turned to look at Katherine. She was stirring her Cape Cod with the swizzle stick absentmindedly, still staring down at the face of the jukebox. Her stirring motions were jerky. It was obvious she was well on her way to getting drunk.

"Let's sit down," Katherine stated, tearing her gaze from the juke.

"At a table," stopped me in my tracks as I started to head back to the bar. I didn't want to sit at a table - it took too long to get a drink and that's what I had come there for.

"We can talk," she offered in explanation, as if we couldn't talk at the bar.

Maybe she'll have something interesting to say, I hoped. I wasn't in the mood to argue with some girl I'd just met. We went over to the table in the back, against a wall. I took the Gunfighter Seat: back corner chair, facing the front door. I could finally see the TV that was bolted against the wall above the bar. The two old guys were watching some news program on one of those cable channels up around 60, I realized. A camo clad soldier ran by the camera, crouched low behind a bush. I had been wondering what they were watching with the sound off. All this ran through my mind as I sat down. I stared at Katherine for a tense moment.

"What do you do?" I couldn't believe her question.

"I work in a factory making stuff," was my answer. I tried to be as vague as I could. What else did she need to know? The fucking job didn't define who I was. It was something I did to pay the rent and that was it. I almost asked her "What do you do?" but I really didn't want to know.

"What was happening back at that party?" I did ask to break the silence. It was 11:15 p.m. and by my calculations things would be winding down just about then.

"People were leaving," she explained. "I was bored. Marco wanted to go home," she added quickly, almost as an afterthought, forehead creasing. So that's his name.

"That party was lame," went my statement, "and there is no greater sin than being boring."

I wanted to ask her who Marco was but decided against it. What the fuck did I want to know that for? Only complicate things. "Man, what was wrong with those guys back there?" I asked, vaguely interested.

Katherine launched into the tale of how she knew the host and hostess, that began with, "When Marco used to work with..."

I followed the cadence of her voice, nodding my head 'yes' at the appropriate moments, not really listening. My attention wandered over to the siren song of that silent TV set. It briefly held the image of a dead peasant laying face down in a muddy ditch until the picture changed to a rooftop view of a typical third world city. The dateline read Lima, Peru.

I realized it was a news broadcast about the Sendero Luminoso. Basically, there was a civil war going on in Peru and it was the government against the Sendero Luminoso with the native Indios caught in the middle. Sendero Luminoso means Shining Path. They're Maoist guerrillas who believe the only way to save Peru is to bring the country to its knees and rebuild from the rubble. They figure that if you make the masses miserable enough they'll rise up in revolt. Well, they had pretty much succeeded - in making the masses miserable, that is. The government may have controlled the major cities but the Senderos pretty much owned the hills and seemed able to kill power stations, water treatment plants, radio stations, and anything or anybody else that offended them, at will. The government responded in kind. It was a sad state of affairs.

Liberating an entire country seemed like a tall order to me. I was thinking more on a personal level. I lapsed into another daydream. It would have been dope to get up on the roof of my apartment with a deer rifle and maybe free up the corner of McAllister and Steiner. Liberate the block even. You know, a hail of lead, lone gunman issues crazy demands, tense standoff situation. Alive, screaming, on top of the world and looking down on creation. Right before police snipers cut you down like a dog.

I realized Katherine's voice had trailed off in a question as I sat there eyeing the TV set. I tore my gaze back to hers. She obviously expected some sort of answer but I had no idea what the fuck she was talking about. I'd had enough though.

"Hey, man," I offered. "Let's get out of here."

"Yeah," Katherine smiled. Her hands made a confused motion as if they were going to check her pockets but didn't. Damn, that last drink sure climbed on her back.

I stood, leaving my empty beer bottle on the table. Katherine followed suit. By the time I pushed my way out the doors, my jacket was on and buttoned. I thrust my hands deep into my pants' pockets against the cold. There were a couple of coins in the right one and I closed my fingers around them trying to discern their denomination by touch. I could tell by their rough edges that some of the bigger discs were quarters. About a buck twenty in change, I figured.

I stopped on the sidewalk in front of The Embers to wait for

Katherine. She was right behind me. I realized it was time to say my goodbyes. Cut loose the dead weight.

"Hey, Katherine," I tried to start off easily. "I'm gonna head home. I'll see you around." Maybe if I ended on a light note she wouldn't trip.

"How are you getting home?" Katherine asked.

"Good question," was my answer.

"I'm taking the N-Judah," she said coyly. "You could walk me home."

Never let it be said that I was callous enough to throw a girl to the wolves. Just say I was too stupid to see it coming.

We waited at the streetcar stop on Irving and 7th. I stared up into the sky trying to figure which constellation was which. It used to really bug me. I could never see anything but a bunch of random patterns. It was like I was too stupid to make out Orion's Belt, the Little Dipper or anything. Katherine hummed a song under her breath. I didn't recognize the tune.

The N-Judah came finally. I almost couldn't bear the silence anymore. We boarded and Katherine flashed her transit pass. I dug in my pockets for the 85 cents. We took a seat in the back, two of the only riders on the train. I was tempted not to sit next to her but did so anyway. Katherine started to tell me more about herself. I stared out of the window trying not to listen. Finally I didn't want to hear it anymore so I asked her how far she was going.

"This is it," she stated, blinking in surprise. We got off on the corner of Carl and Cole. She pointed to a window on the third story of an apartment building across the street.

"That's our apartment," Katherine informed me.

"Huh?!" I looked at her. I thought she wanted someone to escort her home so she wouldn't get jumped. Katherine rummaged around in her jacket pockets, slightly uncoordinated. She was definitely drunk. I wondered what she was looking for.

"Here's my number at work. Give me a call sometime," she said in a low voice, holding out a small rectangle of stiff paper.

I crammed her business card into my pocket without bothering to look at it. I realized how close Katherine was standing to me. Maybe it was my imagination but it didn't seem like she was that close a moment before. She leaned forward and with her right hand on the back of my neck, pulled my lips to her. I resisted slightly. The force of her clutch mashed my mouth against hers. One of her top teeth split my lip. I tasted my own blood. She tried to jam her tongue between my teeth. I yanked my head back with a jerk. Katherine smiled in satisfaction, opening her eyes. Figured she'd roped another one.

"Marco's waiting up for me," she motioned to the lit window with her head.

I couldn't fucking believe it. How could someone be that cruel and heartless? It was unbelievable to me. We were standing right under their bedroom window but here I was.

"I better let you go then," I said in a voice I thought was dripping with sarcasm. Katherine must have mistaken it for jealousy.

"Call me," she promised. Staring me in the eye the whole time, she turned, looking over her shoulder and walked up the front steps to the apartment. It was done slowly, just for my benefit. I watched the whole thing in disbelief.

"Call me," Katherine repeated before disappearing.

I started off down the block, jamming my hands back into my pockets. Her card was in the left one. My hand closed around it. I still couldn't believe it. The whole scene had a surreal quality to it that I'd come to appreciate. How could she do that? Didn't her conscience bother her? Just when I thought I'd seen it all.

I mean, sure, it was flattering but the last thing I needed was to get hooked up with someone like that. I knew it was hypocritical of me but how could I trust her? I mean, what was going to stop me from being the next Marco?

Familiarity breeds contempt. Suddenly the awful truth pounded in my empty skull. I was killing myself with this bullshit. All the hurt feelings and lies. It was time to simplify things. Even if I did find Her, things could never be the same. She wouldn't be the same and even though I still felt like a lump of human shit, I wasn't the same either. There were too many miles and too much time between us. It was time to live my own life.

Unconsciously I had been crumpling Katherine's business card into a little ball in my pocket. It was the size of a pea and pretty tight by then. I made my decision before even being conscious of it. I jerked my hand out of its pocket and flicked the card out into the street. It sailed across the cone of light cast by the street light and disappeared into the darkness on the other side. I felt better immediately. Like that one action had set me on a new course. I walked home feeling okay.

Shit, there is even a beer waiting for me in the refrigerator behind the milk, I was thinking.

P.S. Got home just in time to see my roommate finish that last beer.

Kick It Down

Practically every young man attempted to acquire some personal power that would serve his own interests. As with Medicine Men, such personal power could be achieved through a vision quest. The young man would go off by himself for several days to a high hill, fasting, searching, seeking some relationship between himself and nature. If he was fortunate, he would have a dream in which a spirit would reveal certain sacred objects or designs that would bring supernatural aid in times of need.

— *The Indians* by Benjamin Capps
(Time-Life Books, New York, 1973)

I reluctantly start to drift back into consciousness, out of the blackness, thinking about the Ohlones. It has something to do with a book I read for an oral report in the fifth grade, but for the life of me, I can't remember much. Only this one passage that keeps repeating over and over in the darkness inside of my head like a broken record. My senses are slow in coming back to me but they begin to reassert themselves.

I'm lying face down with the dry, flinty smell of sand in my nostrils. The flat sand is hardpacked, unyielding to the weight of my body. My mouth is dry and sticky. A gust of wind blows over me. I feel my body jump and shiver but my mind is too detached to register the cold. It's far away, cocooned in the soothing darkness.

One arm is twisted underneath me but the throbbing pain is too remote to be noticeable. It's just another nagging sensation tugging at the periphery of my awareness. It's too much effort to open my eyes, let alone move, so I lay here and listen to the rhythm of small shore waves breaking. Their sound comes in with a soothing consistency that slowly lulls me back down into the nothingness. I am tired. Occasionally the rumble of a big wave crashing farther out brings me up out of the dark and I catch a whiff of barbecue smoke.

I can just imagine some overweight family of four from Castro Valley impatiently crowded around their hibachi as the coals smolder. This is their first summer visit to Ocean Beach and their pale flesh is sunburned when even briefly exposed to the sun's mild rays. My mind passes over their bloated faces as they watch the fire's progress. I have almost mentally constructed their pudgy little hands ravenously tearing into bleeding pieces of undercooked meat when the roar of a larger wave pulls me up closer to the surface. I can feel the surf pound the beach through my bones.

How the fuck did I get here, I ask myself. I begin wondering what I'm doing at the beach. Frankly, the beach sucks. Nothing but jarheads, WPODs (white punks on dope), and no-necks. Worst of all are the women. The thought of being scoped out by females makes my skin crawl. There is nothing worse than having someone's mother, or little sister for that matter, give you the once over twice. Besides, I'm not what you would call 'buff'. Ha, far from it.

Maybe if I could remember how it all started. I guess it's best to start at the beginning, but somehow I always come in clueless somewhere in the middle. Used to bug the shit out of me. I couldn't get the dream out of my head. Sometimes, when I was waking up, I couldn't be sure it didn't really happen, like a premonition or a half-forgotten memory.

Anyway, in my dream my father would come into my old bedroom late at night. He stood just inside the doorway, framed by the rectangle of light coming through my open door. His face was hidden in the shadows by the glare coming from the hall but I could tell it was my father by the plaid shirt. He had this favorite red and black Pendleton he always wore around the house. He would just stand there and stare at me, stand and stare.

I was small, maybe five years old again. The single bed stretched out before me, huge. I lay there paralyzed, impotent, too terrified to speak. It was infuriating. Finally, he would turn around and walk away without saying a word. It was as if he silently passed judgment on me there in the dark and found me wanting. A few years ago I realized he really wasn't coming back, and I haven't dreamed about him since.

I was about six when it happened but can still vaguely remember the whole episode. I was confined to the inside of the house with the flu, secluded from the pouring rain and the neighborhood kids stomping in the overflowing gutters. It was Saturday and I had spent most of my morning laying on the couch under an itchy blanket, watching cartoons in between coughing fits. I couldn't smell anything. My nose had been running mercilessly for the last two days. The nostrils were red and chafed from constantly wiping the freely flowing snot. My clogged ears throbbed with the noise of their argument.

They had been fighting all morning. About what, I didn't know and it didn't matter. If they didn't have something to squabble over they would find or invent something. Suburban cabin fever. Their screams increased in volume and intensity along with my fright. I was too young to understand why they were hurting each other. Finally, I couldn't stand anymore so I went into the kitchen.

My father was gripping my mother's arms, shouting, "I can't trust you! You never believed in me!" in her face. A vein throbbed alarmingly on either side of his neck and his bright red face looked swollen with anger ready to explode.

My mother was sobbing, "Leave me alone. I just want to go," over and over, her head hanging down.

I shrieked, "Stop it, stop it!" and began to cry.

As my father turned to look at me, my mother broke free and ran out of the house. They always had these types of arguments.

My father would go off, saying things he didn't mean, later regretting them. My mother couldn't deal, she kept her feelings inside. The old man took one good look at me and I guess something snapped.

He went into their room, threw some shit into an old suitcase we had, climbed into his brown LTD and drove away. I sat on the kitchen floor, crying hysterically, waiting for someone to come home, anyone. I was alone inside the house for what seemed like hours. I convinced myself that I had been abandoned. My tears came in long wracked sobs. Finally, my mother came back soaked. She had been walking in the rain. My father never came back. A couple of months later we moved to the city. I guess my mom got sick of waiting for that old brown LTD to show up.

Anyway, in my dream, the adults were standing, towering over me, impossibly tall. I must have been too small to be noticeable because they were talking about me as if I wasn't there. That was when I realized I was strapped down, naked, to the top of my little desk like it was some sort of operating table. Painfully bright lights shone down into my eyes but I couldn't turn my head out of the glare because of the strap cinched tightly across my forehead.

Huge faces were crowded around the table peering down intently. They reached forward and took turns tearing me open with their bare hands. I could feel those hands ripping out huge chunks, their fingers entwined in my intestines, pulling. Fascinated, they scrutinized each bloody handful. Everyone was speaking at once, drowning each other out so I could only make out brief snatches of what each was saying, like some crazy, tossed, word salad.

"...severely limited attention span," said Mrs. Matselboba.

"...dysfunctional family environment only perpetuates the downward spiral," I caught my mother saying.

"...extremely uncooperative, classic antisocial tendencies," added the crossing guard lady.

"...inferior...," my father summed it up.

I wanted to say something but nothing would come out of my dumb stricken mouth. As they stepped back to admire their handiwork, their hands dripping blood, I got a chance to look down.

My stomach looked like it had exploded outwards. The intestines hung in bloody ropes and I could see my heart beat faintly through the shattered rib cage. I felt the vomit claw its way up my throat. They must not have been done because the bloody hands reached for my face, intending to complete the autopsy, see if they could find anything in my hollow head. I wrenched open my mute lips to scream something, anything, when a high pitched shrieking painfully filled my head and startled me awake.

I tore my bloodshot eyes open. I had been drooling and was covered in sweat. The first thing I saw was my digital alarm clock. It was on. I could vaguely hear the incessant babble of KGO talk radio from it. I listened to KGO at night when I had trouble falling asleep. Next to it was a green 40-ounce bottle of Mickey's with an inch of flat malt liquor left in the bottom, resting on the nightstand. I couldn't remember how it or the crumpled Big Grab bag of Lay's Potato Chips had gotten there. My stomach remembered the dream on its own and convulsed at the gory memory. A combo of acidic bile and metallic blood tastes elbowed their way into my mouth. It felt like there was an angry demon in my stomach with a red hot fire poker.

I'm barely nineteen, I thought to myself as I desperately tried to swallow. I can't feel like this already.

My room had the shut-in smell of a night of drunken sleep, all alcohol vapors and heavy breathing. The shrill ring of the phone assaulted my aching ears again as I fought down the urge to puke. I could see the phone on the kitchen table from where I lay doubled up on the bed. It was one of those cheap plastic phones they sell at the flea market, shaped like a mallard. My mother loved it, she was crazy for ducks like that. We had duck paraphernalia littering the place. I had to suppress the urge to smash the phone into as many pieces as I could every time I saw it. I yanked myself out of bed to stop the high-pitched, screeching ring.

"What happened last night?" I asked myself as I picked my way across the cluttered floor. I was supposed to go over to Lindsey's but went out with Mike, Scott and Brent first. I reached the phone before any conclusion.

"Hello?" croaked out of my paste-covered throat, surprising myself.

"Kurt Richard, you're still asleep," my mother's voice accused.

"No, Mom," I lied. I quickly added, "I was just getting up," to alleviate my guilty conscience by making my statement a half-truth (or a half-lie, depending on how you looked at it). I sat down at the kitchen table. The vinyl seat cushion felt cold against the back of my thighs.

"You're gonna be late for that dead-end job," she started in. She was right, according to the cheap duck motif clock on the kitchen wall.

"You're right," I replied, trying to end this conversation we had been having practically every morning for the last year and a half. "I'd better get going."

Man, I was exhausted. I never woke up feeling refreshed even after six or seven hours of serious down time. It was like I never fell asleep. I was stumbling through life perpetually haggard.

"Kurt, don't you want to make me proud of you?" she pleaded with me.

Now that really pissed me off. What the fuck did I care what the bitch thought of me - she was my mother, after all. Wasn't she supposed to love me no matter how much of a drunken fuck-up I was? How could I tell her that I had no idea what I wanted to do with my life? I only knew what I didn't want to do.

I wasn't a 'people person' (come to think of it, I hated them), I had a problem with authority figures, no formal occupational training, and I didn't know anyone 'in the business'. Basically, I was Rat-Fucked. I could sum up my whole pathetic life in one simple sentence and it was a run-on.

I worked as a busboy at the downtown Zim's and almost liked the job in a masochistic way. The mindless tedium of clearing endless, cluttered tables seemed to free up my brain. I could step back and look at my life from the position of a neutral third party. Even though I never came to any real conclusion, except in that I was miserable, I didn't give up hope. Something had to be done, I just hadn't figured out what yet. At least I wasn't one of the old Mexican dudes washing dishes.

Don't get me wrong, it wasn't like I felt superior to them or anything. Just the opposite, I respected them for just trying to get by, never having it easy, being outsiders. Somehow, through all the bullshit they had never lost their dignity. They were helping me with my Spanish, only having taken the two mandatory years necessary for high school graduation and I guess, conversely, I was helping them with their English.

Me, Taurino, Mauro, and Efraim would bullshit in the kitchen when things were slow: threaten each other with knives, brag about our previous night's drinking, that kind of shit. They called me 'El Mojado' even though they knew I was only a half-breed, born right here in the U.S. of A., but it was a nice compliment. The irony of it made them laugh.

"You could sign up for classes at City College again," the old lady went on nevertheless. "Spring quarter just began."

"Mom," I interrupted before she got a chance to get any farther, "I tried that and it was no good, remember? Two months. Like grade thirteen. I dropped out before getting kicked out. I dug my grave and now I gotta lie in it."

I was so sick of this conversation that I went for the throat. This stopped my mother but I could hear her office coworkers in the background chime in with such helpful hints as "Skyline just started a couple of days ago," and "I hear City College offers tutors."

"Look," I sighed, "I better get going."

"Okay," she sighed disappointedly, "I love you."

Now why did she have to go and say that? My stomach sunk as I hung up the phone. I felt guilty for losing patience with the old lady but she sure knew how to push my buttons. Anyway, I knew my wasted life would become their topic of choice for the rest of the morning, again.

Let me make my own mistakes. The thought of those losers critiquing my life really pissed me off. I had this vision of me walking into her office and telling Lloyd, Rose, Earl, and Susan that they were dead from the waist down. Grey, inanimate dolls with no sex drive and less will to live. I could imagine their surprised faces as I let them know they were just waiting to be buried.

Any pleasure I had gotten from my daydream disappeared as I realized that they weren't maliciously interfering with my life. In fact, just the opposite, they wanted to help. They knew what it was all about. The thought of their dead-end lives and ruined dreams made me feel really depressed. I didn't want, ask for, or need their help, but they felt compelled to offer their pitiful observations.

I was absentmindedly staring down at the kitchen table during this emotional rollercoaster. In the center of my field of vision, on top of that morning's already read newspaper, was my mother's overflowing ashtray. It was her favorite, the one she had stolen from the Mallard Club. There were about eight butts piled up from the cigarettes she had smoked last night after work, stained with her pink lipstick. On top were balanced the three she'd had with breakfast, unstained. I stared down blankly at the carcinogenic pyramid before me. Next to it was a hand.

My right hand, I realized. The knuckles were crisscrossed with a fine lace of small cuts. A little blood had pooled up and dried in the crease between my index and pointer fingers. I had no clue as to what had happened. I stared down in detached wonder for a couple of seconds.

My head throbbed, I shuddered, and this broke me out of it. I quickly looked back at the duck clock. My stomach contracted as I realized she was right, I was going to be late. Jesus Christ, I couldn't believe the pain as my gut knotted itself into a ball. The cramp formed deep within my bowels, then doubled.

"Gotta make it to the bathroom," I pleaded with myself. I stood up, clenched my butt cheeks and waddled into the bathroom. Never mind shutting the door, no one was home anyway. I ripped down my boxers and sat on the toilet in one hurried motion. God, it felt good. The knot loosened a little as I let go.

It was one of those fluffy beer shits, all foam and potato chips that keeps coming and coming. I sat with my head in my hands feeling better by the second. Wiped my ass once, twice, and a third time just to make sure. I yanked up my boxers and looked down into the bowl like everybody does before flushing. A spot of blood floated in the bowl, submerged just under the surface like a small crimson flower blossom. Oh man, not again, I thought to myself.

I had seen this before. It meant I wasn't taking very good care of myself. Far from it. If I wasn't careful I would end up with an ulcer. Be one of those guys constantly gulping Maalox. Permanent Rolaids chalk breath. Hunched over because the pain in their gut is caving their chest in. I vowed not to go out like that and promised to take better care of myself. If I had some sort of health insurance I could get that spot of blood checked out by a professional.

I did a quick brush of my film-covered teeth, gagged, and looked in the mirror. Ran my hands through my hair a couple of times as I stared at my face. God, I looked terrible. I had huge bags under red-rimmed eyes, sleep biscuits still caked in the corners. My big nose hooked to the left from the time I broke it in high school. I caught an elbow in PE playing basketball, blood everywhere. I wouldn't go to the nurse because I didn't want to admit that my nose was broken. Those guys used to give me enough shit about the size of my beak as it was, I couldn't give them that satisfaction. Never did get it set. I still hate that fucking game. Miles had given me this jacked-up, flat top crewcut in his mother's kitchen last week. My curly brown hair was shorn close to the skull. Freckles. Otherwise average. No identifying scars, tattoos, or deformities. I didn't recognize the face staring back at me, but who ever does?

I shuffled into my room to get dressed. My black work slacks, apron, and white shirt were lying in a tangled heap at the foot of the bed where I had thrown them the night before. The bow tie was still clipped to the shirt's rumpled collar. As I pulled this ensemble on for the third morning in a row, I hoped again that good ol' Art Kane wouldn't notice the wrinkled, lint-covered state of my uniform, again. Man, I hated that maggot. Greasy blonde hair parted perfectly down the middle like it had been done with a protractor.

Hadn't that bullshit gone out with the '70s?

Cheesy mustache. Close set pig eyes. 5'4", little man's complex. You know the type. I could barely stand to look at him. I guess the feeling was mutual because he was always fucking with me. Somehow I had become the unofficial Zim's scapegoat. Art seemed to radar in on me as soon as I came in late, hungover, or both, which was a majority of the time. Kane never got sick of his "If you can't take this job seriously..." speech, which he practiced on me constantly. It was almost as if he thought he would finally get it right and I would be miraculously transformed into the ideal employee by that tired monologue.

I mean, I wasn't even a full-time employee. I was still considered part-time (even though I usually worked six days a week, forty plus hours) because I was on a rotating shift. That way Kane didn't have to justify the expense of another person receiving a decent salary, overtime, or benefits. It wasn't like it came out of his pockets or anything, he was only the manager. He just got enjoyment out of pushing people around. Must have gotten fucked with a lot in junior high and high school. Now he had his chance to wield a little power and it had gone to his head. Probably had rationalized it all out to himself. Payback is a bitch.

Last week Kane had gotten some wild hair up his ass about the stockroom needing a thorough cleaning. I mean, sure it was filthy and all, but no more so than the bathrooms, behind the counter, or the whole place for that matter. That kind of deep-fried squalor stays with a place no matter what you do. If he really wanted the place clean we should have gone in with flame-throwers. Scorched earth policy. Started over from the ground up.

Anyway, my job was to take everything off the shelves, wipe them down, and put it all back. Sound simple? Only in theory. The grime on the bottoms of the boxes had other ideas. To make this exercise in futility even more enjoyable, Art wanted all the heavy stuff (industrial size canned foods and jugs of dishwasher detergent) on the top shelves and the light stuff (napkins and plastic forks) on the bottom. Perfectly arranged to kill some poor, unsuspecting sap.

I didn't plan on sticking around long enough for it to be me. However, not knowing what kind of fucked up task was waiting for me kind of made the job interesting. It was like a challenge to make it through the shift with that asshole constantly lording over me.

Man, I hate that anal retentive fuckhead! I thought to myself as I slammed the front door to the house.

I frantically rammed my right hand, in search of keys, into my empty pants' pockets. I had walked out of the house once again without keys, money, or wallet.

"Shit, I'm locked out!" I screamed, stating the obvious.

My left hand was occupied, at that moment, with my breakfast: an old plastic 7-11 *Indiana Jones and the Temple of Doom* cup, three-quarters full of cold black coffee the Mister Coffee had made the old lady this morning, to which I had added four heaping teaspoons of sugar. We were out of milk. I took a couple of hesitant steps in opposite directions on the porch not knowing quite what to do. The stench of wet, rotting garbage assaulted my big nose. There was a small room under the front stairs for the garbage cans. When it rained the porch leaked into the cans. Perfect breeding ground for microbial fermentation. Weren't they supposed to come pick that shit up yesterday, I asked myself.

Oh well, fucked again. You get used to it.

I stumbled down the stairs and barely managed to grab the handrail in time to save myself. My breakfast, however, tried to bum rush the far rim of the cheap plastic 7-11 *Indiana Jones and the Temple of Doom* cup. This I quickly negotiated with a deft flick of the wrist that gave the rebounding wave of coffee the critical amount of extra energy necessary to jump the opposite lip of the cup.

My body reflexively stiffened with the slosh of cold, and I almost threw my cheap plastic 7-11 *Indiana Jones and the Temple of Doom* cup into the street, but stopped myself with the realization of two important facts:

    1) It could have been hot; and

    2) I wasn't going to get anything else for breakfast.

I shuffled off down the street gulping at my breakfast and trying to piece together my jagged memories of the night before.

It had been Valentine's Day. I didn't know why that struck me as funny. I was gonna go by Lindsey's after work to give her a card I'd picked up at the last minute. I was walking into #1 Super Markette for some beer, when Sam reminded me that it was Valentine's Day. Sam was the Persian owner of the neighborhood liquor store. He had been there since we had moved onto the block and insisted we call him Sam from the start. I had been going to his store for, like, nine years and I still wasn't sure what his real name was. He claimed the Persian was too hard to pronounce, but I got the impression that he was ashamed of it. I didn't know why, probably no dumber a name than the rest of them we're branded with at birth. I mean, come on, Sam.

Anyway, Sam was the coolest. Somehow he managed to stay about two to three years behind in fashion. Sam had just gotten heavily into Acid Wash. Overalls, shirt, hat... you name it. It was only a matter of time before he jumped on the lycra bandwagon. The thought of him in some neon bike shorts used to kill me.

He kept his greasy black hair combed straight back, and I don't think I ever saw him without at least two gold chains nestled in his thick chest hair. Anyway, some of the guys hated Sam, they called him The Shah, but he had always been cool with me. He didn't card me for beer even though he knew I wasn't twenty-one.

They complained to me, "Man, denied by The Shah again," when he wouldn't let them buy up. Like it was gonna help, bitching to me. I knew a good thing when I saw it. It was Sam's brother, Merdad, I couldn't stand. He never liked me from day one. Merdad would always start loudly talking shit in Farsii, or Hindu, or whatever it is that they speak, about me the minute I set foot in the door. Man, fuck that guy.

The best part was, I usually ignored him and talked to Sam as if he wasn't there. That pissed Merdad off to no end, but gave me much satisfaction. I always wanted to ask Sam how to say "Suck-a-dick" in Farsii/Hindu, but didn't want to cause him any grief.

When Sam asked, "What have you got your woman for Valentine's Day?" all I could do was groan. How the fuck could I forget something like that?

It's not like they don't start with the Valentine's Day advertising on January 1st for just that reason. Sam was pleased to point out his vast selection of timely greeting cards, strategically arranged on a rack in front of the cash register. I tried to choose the least sappy of the remaining three cards but ended up with a picture of a dozen long stemmed roses and the inscription, My Most Beautiful Valentine. It was either that or a choice between a Holly Hobby-esque card with two goofy cartoon kids holding hands and one that began To My Loving Wife.... Grim choices.

I had wandered down Fulton a couple of blocks without making any real headway. What had happened last night?

I had a nagging sensation I was missing something just out of reach of my faltering memory. All I needed to do was concentrate harder and it might come. My eyes were looking down, scrutinizing my falling feet. I've always hated the way I walk. A crazy shuffle with a rhythm that changes every couple of yards. I've never found a style I'm comfortable with. My gait is so bad sometimes that my hips begin to ache after six or seven blocks. I jerked my gaze upwards as I passed into the cold shadow of the freeway overpass. 101 crossed over Fulton down by Gough. I was halfway to work when I passed under that dirty freeway.

Shit! I was startled. I had almost ran into this guy. He stood silently about a step and a half ahead in the middle of the sidewalk. Seemed like he was waiting for me. At first I thought it was just some old vagrant propped up in a crusty old overcoat (was it originally black or had the succession of nights spent sleeping in the scum of downtown doorways stained it that shade?) when I looked into his crazy eyes.

Piercing blue irises drowning in a swamp of jaundiced cornea. I was trapped by his intently staring eyes like a rat hypnotized by a hungry snake. Liver spots dotted the dirty scalp at the edge of his receding hairline. His long hair hung in greasy clumps pushed back from the sloping forehead. A thick layer of dirt was ground into the skin of his face and hands, giving them a dead, leathery look. The cracks and wrinkles of that weather-beaten mug were etched in black grime.

His eyes narrowed as the mouth split into a grin. The lips kept pulling back further, and further, and further, until I was sure his head would split. His smile was pulled taut over yellow teeth and bleeding gums. The gums had receded, drawn so far back that his teeth resembled huge stained and pitted ivory tusks. Decay had engraved its twisted path across the ruined enamel like illegible hieroglyphics. What story did they tell?

I couldn't believe the size of those teeth. How the fuck did they all fit inside that mouth, like some godforsaken human piranha? I stared into the mouth, fascinated. A film of crust had filled the gap between a canine and eye tooth, and a fleck of spit was caught way up in the corner of that huge mouth.

"I been watching you, boy," hissed the mouth.

I realized it was right, he had been. Sometimes I gave some of my change to the bums who slept in the parking lot under the freeway. The ground stayed relatively dry and the cops rarely fucked with them, as long as they were gone before the first commuters came.

The Leprechaun was my favorite: small build, big red nose, long brown beard, green felt hat. He hung out in the Civic Center pavilion during the day and was usually fucked by noon. I liked the guy, he spent his earnings on Milwaukee's Best. I vaguely remembered The Mouth, standing back, never asking for the inevitable spare change. Always grinning that huge, terrible smile, the yellow eyes just watching.

"I...," I began, not knowing what to say, my voice trailing off. I was terrified. What did he mean? The Mouth hissed his decaying laugh in my face. I choked on the stench. His eyes peered intently into mine, bright with insanity. The forest was on fire behind those pupils.

Desperately, I pushed past him. All I wanted to do was get away from The Mouth, any thought of work forgotten. I couldn't help but do a quick double take to see if he was right behind me, but The Mouth stood rooted to the middle of the sidewalk grinning that awful crocodile smile. I didn't know what he meant, but it gave me a paranoid, creepy feeling. I half turned and looked back over my shoulder just to be sure The Mouth wasn't coming after me. Like the Cheshire Cat, I could see his grin halfway down the block. What the fuck was that all about?

I don't need this spooky shit, I thought as I turned down Van Ness. The wind blew out of the gray February sky and up Van Ness like a trash-strewn wind tunnel. Test the air drag coefficient of the average weekday *San Francisco Chronicle* some day. I stuck my hands into my jacket pockets and pulled my Derby tighter around me as an empty Burger King bag flew past my shins. I think what bothered me most was that The Mouth seemed vaguely familiar. I was wracking my addled memory when I realized I was in front of Zim's plate glass windows. Back to the salt mines, as the old lady would say.

I was late and I fucking knew it. I wondered if I should just keep on going. Go back to the house and get back in bed, maybe pick up a six-pack on the way. Sounded like a good idea, maybe a couple of hours of sleep was all I needed, but my momentum carried me in the front doors. Dianne, the head waitress of the shift (as if there was such a thing as a 'head waitress' - she had just been there the longest and bitched the most) gave me her patented 'you're in trouble now' look. Shit, I was late already, might as well do some reconnaissance.

"Is ALF looking for me?" I asked Dianne, looking around guiltily. We all had nicknames for Kane, my personal favorite being ALF: Arrogant Little Fucker, followed in a close second by The Weasel. That's when I saw her again.

Brunette, sitting perfectly, ramrod straight up and down like she owned the place. She had been coming in for the last three days at 11:38 a.m. like clockwork, today being no exception. It started Tuesday.

I noticed a well dressed women in her thirties, sitting alone, having an early lunch. The only reason she registered at all (we get plenty of business women eating lunch alone and I can't stand that uptight/frigid/holier-than-thou type) was that the bitch kept staring at me. I didn't know what the fuck she saw (was I bleeding from the scalp?) but it made me hell of uncomfortable. I could feel her eyes burning a hole in the back of my head while I cleared off tables. Even then she scrutinized me coldly through some expensive looking sunglasses.

I wanted to scream, "What are you looking at bitch?!"

"He's always looking for you," Dianne replied. Her comment snapped me out of my daze.

I hope the Weasel is in his office, I thought as I hurried back to the dingy break/coat room. With any luck I could stash the 7-11 *Indiana Jones and the Temple of Doom* cup, get my apron on, and be clearing off a table before Kane noticed how late I was. No such luck. The bastard was waiting for me in the hall.

"Late again, Kurt?" he asked sarcastically.

Depends if you round up or down, I could almost hear myself say.

"If you can't take this job seriously...," ALF began, working himself up to the frenzy necessary for a full blown lecture. Jesus Christ, I'll spontaneously combust if I hear this tired bullshit one more time. Did I say that?

"Art, the reason I'm late...," I began lamely, trying desperately to think of some excuse.

Man, this bullshit used to particularly annoy the fuck out of me. They didn't close until 9 p.m., so I ended up staying an extra unpaid fifteen minutes while they locked up every night anyway. What the fuck did he care if I was late a few minutes every once in a while? Okay, regularly. Nevertheless, here I was, once again trying to come up with a new excuse.

"No excuses," he sighed, annoyed, as if he'd finally realized the futility of another lecture. He paused for a second, not really knowing what to do. We stood there lamely.

"The women's bathroom needs mopping," burst out of his mouth suddenly. The thought of this particularly gruesome task seemed to cheer him up. "The toilet overflowed this morning. Someone's got to clean it up."

"Sure, no problem," I muttered. God, I hated myself. That motherfucker had saved this bullshit for me to clean up. "You'll get yours, Mussolini," I said to the hunched shoulders as they disappeared into the dining area.

I went to the storage area and got the mop and bucket. One of the first 'Special Projects' I got when I started there was to mop behind the counter. Man, I couldn't believe the threadbare condition of the mop then. I doubted that it really did anything but push the dirt around, but it wasn't like I was gonna go to all the trouble to find a new mop head or nothing. I mean, 'You pay peanuts, you get monkeys'. The hot bleach water in the bucket turned dark gray with the first dunk of that dingy mop.

I knew this job sucked, but at least it meant that I got to kick back in there undisturbed. I mean, who's gonna fuck with a guy cleaning out a backed-up toilet, for godsakes? It was kind of cool. The idea of 'their' bathroom had intrigued me for I don't know how long. What made it so different from a men's room? Initially, I thought it was the fact that there weren't any urinals to piss in, but that was too obvious. As I mopped the floors it occurred to me. The hostility was absent or at least subdued.

The angry graffiti concerning cock size and sexual preference was missing. No broken tile or chipped sinks. It was even kind of clean, but it still smelled like a bathroom. The thought of them locked inside that room doing something mysterious and feminine was kind of exciting. I had spread gray bleach water around the floor under the sinks and was starting under the toilet when I heard the bathroom door being pushed open.

"I'm mopping in here. Be done in a minute," I called out in a sing-song voice over my shoulder without looking.

"I know," I heard her say as she stepped in.

I stood bolt upright and turned to look at her. She had pushed those expensive sunglasses up onto her head. They pulled her long dark hair back over pearl-studded ears. Her brown eyes, edged with hazel, looked straight into mine. They were absolutely white, not a trace of bloodshot. A few freckles scattered across high cheekbones. She had a good strong nose, giving her face character. A couple of lines ran across her forehead but otherwise wrinkle-free. She was beautiful. I noticed she had undone her blouse a button. I could just catch a hint of black lace. Freckles dotted the tanned chest and a thin gold chain hung about her elegant neck.

She gave me a look I was meant to feel in my right hip pocket. You know the one. Her eyes widened and she looked deeply, dreamily into mine. What's up with that bullshit? I hate it. Am I supposed to go weak in the knees and become a willing love slave just because some bitch threw her mojo bedroom eyes at me?

"I've been watching you, young man," her full, red lips said.

I flinched and half expected her head to be torn open by an impossibly large grin filled with ravenous teeth. The mask would fall away, revealing the rotting old hag underneath. She mistook my shock for fear and smiled. "Don't worry, they won't find us," she said, leaning back and closing the door.

I heard the lock click. The smell of her expensive perfume rode in on my gasp of surprise. I didn't recognize the scent, but that didn't surprise me, since I was able to identify only one perfume by name: Love's Baby Soft. I wondered who she meant by 'they'. Probably caused part of the excitement.

She crossed the bathroom in three slow steps as I stood dumbfounded, staring at her. Something about the sultry way she walked aroused me. A red lacquered fingernail scraped gently along my forearm as she walked around me painfully slowly. Her breath was right in my ear, I could feel it on the back of my neck and on my cheek as she completed one full revolution. She stopped in front of me, standing very, very close and stared up into my face. Again with that fucking wide-eyed mojo love look.

She smiled sensuously, arched her back and began "I want...," in a husky voice.

She never got to tell me what it was. I heard the doorknob turn before I saw the motion. The door shook as someone tried the lock, more violently the second time. I knew it was Kane before the inevitable knock. Three staccato raps on the thin plywood door echoed off the dingy tile as I turned back to look at her. She was still looking at the door. Probably weighing her options.

"Open the door this instant," screamed Kane's muffled voice as he began beating on the door. He must have thought he finally caught me fucking around in a big way, because his annoyed tone actually had a gleeful edge. Probably thought he had nailed me jacking off in the women's bathroom.

"I guess I should open the door," I said lamely. I had a knack for stating the obvious. Two steps carried me over to the door and two fingers unlocked the doorknob. It twisted under my hand.

"I don't know what the fuck you're doing in here but I can't tolerate..." The Weasel pushed his way in, mouth falling open in mid-sentence. "I, uh...," he sputtered, quickly glancing at me, then her, then back at me.

Kane fell silent, not quite knowing what to say. This wasn't what he expected. The three of us stood eyeing each other suspiciously.

"Excuse me," she stated, breaking the awkward silence as she pushed past Kane. He watched her go as I made a hesitant motion towards the mop. ALF turned back before I got there.

"What were you doing in here?" he demanded angrily.

"Nothing," I mumbled, looking down.

"Who do you think you are, locked in the women's restroom with a customer?" he went on regardless.

I didn't dignify that with a response. Just looked him in the eye wearing my best bored expression.

"I've been watching you, Kurt. You have to be the worst employee here. Not only are you habitually late, but now this. I can't get a decent day's work out of you. When are you going to shape up?"

Now, this really irked my ire because I busted ass down there, but what really got to me was the fact that throughout his little tirade he kept spitting on me. Every sentence was punctuated with angry flecks of spittle.

"This isn't working out," he went on in a mock defeated voice. "I thought you could cut it when you started, but I was wrong. You've been a disappointment. I ought to let you go."

Kane obviously wanted me to beg for my job back. With the proper amount of self-deprecation and all around ass-kissing I probably could have gotten it back. Fuck it, that cocksucking job wasn't worth it. That was no fucking way of firing someone. Don't toy with me, motherfucker, I'm not playing that shit. I didn't say anything. We stared at each other.

"You're fired," he finally said.

It was no shock. My days had been numbered from the minute I set foot in that joint. I had realized that a long time before. I just hoped that I would have put a little bit more than the $763.59 away in the bank in my seventeen months of gainful employment before I got the ax. Oh well, that last check would put me somewhere $900. I didn't know what the fuck I was saving for. Ever since I had turned eighteen, I'd had to pay the Old Lady $300 a month for room and board as it was, but I still managed to pigeonhole some of my paycheck away.

"I want to get paid," I snarled. You've got nothing to lose and everything to gain if you're guilty.

"You know payday is next Friday," Kane said in a voice dripping with self-righteous indignation.

Man, fuck that shit, he could go into his office at anytime and cut a check personally. Now I was pissed. I looked that little motherfucker in the eye and paused for a second. My hands clenched into fists unconsciously. Adrenaline OD. I could feel the rush as it hit my bloodstream. The hair on the back of my neck bristled. I had a vision of hauling back and rocking his biscuit. My breath came in deep pants. He got nervous and broke eye contact, looking down.

"I'll be back Monday. I want my check," I spat out between clenched jaws.

I knew I should leave before I did something stupid. I could just imagine cold-cocking Kane and getting arrested for it. The cops would come and take Mr. Manager-Guy's side of the story, me obviously being a drug-addled thug. I would 'resist arrest' and after being properly 'subdued', be led away in cuffs by the shining boys in blue. Book-em-Dano, case closed and cut to commercials. Anyway, it just wasn't worth it, and with that I pushed my way past him.

Okay, so maybe I shouldered him a little harder than I should have, but at that point I really didn't give a fuck. As I grabbed my Derby with the plastic 7-11 *Indiana Jones and the Temple of Doom* cup in the pocket, I couldn't help but notice my hands were shaking. That probably had something to do with the reason my stomach felt like it was full of broken glass.

Anyway, I actually felt a little better as I walked out of that fucking dive. I was finally rid of that albatross around my neck, regardless of the fact that they had fired me. Also the $2.43 in tips that I scooped off the front table on my way out didn't hurt - the price of a 40-ouncer and enough change left over for a phone call to Lindsey.

I looked for the woman from the bathroom on my way out. The table was empty. The only thing left was a crumpled napkin thrown on top of an empty plate. Not even a tip. She must have paid her bill and left in a hurry. Avoid any unpleasantries. Just as well, what the fuck was I gonna say to her?

I fished the change out of my pocket as I approached a phone booth on Van Ness. It seemed like a good time to call Lindsey. She had classes during the morning and would be home by noon. She usually spent the afternoon eating popcorn, doing her homework, and worrying about her weight. I swear she devoted at least four to six hours a day, seven days a week, taking care of her school shit and she still never seemed to finish it all. She would obsess on an assignment days before it was due, claiming complete ignorance and incompetence. Her feelings of frustration and worthlessness would increase geometrically with the onslaught of the due date, until she would finally turn whatever it was in and invariably get an A or at least a high B.

Lindsey worked part time as a waitress at this Italian restaurant in the Sunset, Wednesday through Sunday, from 5 to 10 p.m., so I didn't get to see her until after 11. I usually spent this time drinking a beer and watching her do the rest of her homework. Her parents were always asleep by the time I came over, they had to be up by 5:15 a.m.

Occasionally we talked about her work. You know, work politics. From 'The new girl: can she cut the mustard?' to 'Who's fucking who' to 'I can't stand that bitch'. The weirdest range of topics. I mean, I couldn't understand why the fuck she cared if the boss noticed her hustle or not. Man, a job like that is something you do for the money and anything other than that is for the birds. Lindsey wasn't going to get what she was worth out of them no matter what the fuck she did, so why bother?

Lindsey snatched up the phone on the third ring. "Hello?"

Goddamn, she sounded pissed off already and didn't even know who it was.

"Hey," I tried to ask in an upbeat tone, "Whataya doin'?"

There was a pause. "You bastard," she hissed. "Where's our family portrait?"

Oh shit, it all came back in a flash. I went out with Mike, Scott, and Brent after work the night before. I had learned to drink with these guys. We started with an innocent game of Water Down the Parents' Liquor Cabinet. Drink anything we could sneak out of the house.

I can remember one Saturday afternoon we mixed peppermint schnapps and vodka into a large orange Slurpee. I felt ill and high as a kite. It was great. Soon enough we realized beer was the beverage of choice, and discovered the teenage ritual of 'cornering'. Always a lesson in humility. I'll never forget the night I finished a six-pack to my head without throwing up. I felt like a man, don't ask me why.

We pooled our cash and I was volunteered to score the beer

since I had the connection. #1 Super Markette for three twelve-packs of Milwaukee's Best. Merdad didn't even fuck with me. Just sold me the beer without saying a word. Sam must have spoken to him.

We decided on the Panhandle as the night's spot. There was this little playground we drank at. A park bench to set your beer on, some swings to fuck with later on when you were drunk, and a good stand of trees to use for cover when the cops came, all in that order. I figured I had about an hour and a half of quality time with these bozos and then I'd go see Lindsey. Same old shit with them: drinking, lying, and laughing. Brent was still looking for a job. Had been since I could remember, which wasn't long.

"Thought about applying down at Zim's," he joked, "but I forgot that they only hire women." They all had a chuckle at my expense, Brent's braying laugh drowning everyone else out.

"You'd fit right in," was all I could think of as a comeback, which I said bitterly into my beer.

We began arguing about the dopest way of pulling down a paycheck. Mike was quick to answer, "Valet. You get to dog all those rich motherfuckers' cars."

Mike was like that. Scott opted for bartender on a cruise ship. Obvious line of reasoning: liquor and chicks.

"You wish you were Isaac of *The Love Boat*," we laughed at Scott.

Brent gave it some thought and to his credit, his was the most insipid of them all. If he could have this one wish come true he would be the Night Manager of the Mitchell Bros. Adult Theater.

"Not only do you get to fuck the fresh talent but you can skim money off the top, too." Was that pathetic or what?

"Well?" they all looked at me.

"Huh?" I had no idea. What the fuck? Bank president? Too boring. Dealer? Too risky. Cop? Too macho, besides I couldn't grow a mustache if my life depended on it.

"I... uh... I don't know," I finally had to say.

"Jesus Christ!" Scott said in disgust.

I was on my seventh beer when I noticed the time. 11:19. Shit, late again. It was 11:43 and eight beers down by the time I had walked over to Lindsey's house. The TV was on in the front room, that at least was a good sign. I rang the doorbell and pulled the wrinkled Valentine out of my back pocket. Lindsey opened the door and looked at me but didn't say anything. No sense in trying to kiss her when she was in this kind of mood.

"Hi," I said.

I could barely see the living room behind her, bathed in blue light from the TV. She looked at the Valentine but didn't take it.

"We need to talk," she said, all business.

"Uh, yeah," I replied as I felt my stomach sink and begin to knot. "Can I come in?"

Lindsey stepped out of my way and I followed her into the living room. Shit, here I was late and drunk again. What could I tell her? I was weighing my options as we sat down on the couch. I laid the Valentine down on the coffee table. Lindsey picked up the remote control and turned the volume down on the TV in one fluid motion, all wrist. Damn, she watches a lot of TV.

Lindsey looked at me. I looked at the TV. I could tell she was annoyed. She took a deep breath. I could smell cabbage. Lindsey's mother ate cabbage every night with dinner like clockwork. Said it was good for her heart. Some things never changed.

"Things have changed, Kurt," Lindsey began her little practiced monologue. My head involuntarily turned to look at her. This was a new one. "It's over between us."

She paused. "I want to devote more time to school," Lindsey offered as an excuse.

That was it, I thought to myself. Over in three sentences. Now what the fuck was I supposed to say? Cry? Beg? Try to argue with her? That 'I want to devote more time to school' bit was bullshit. Why not tell me the real reason? Didn't think I could handle it? She'd obviously made up her mind, hence the speech.

It was all too much. Sure I cared for her but how could I tell her that? The last couple of weeks had been strained but no more so than usual. What happened to us? Why now? The unvoiced questions kaleidoscoped in my mind.

"All you ever think about is yourself," she stated.

Do you say that because all I ever do is think about myself, or because I don't think about you, I asked myself.

"I guess I should go then," I said as I stood up.

"Why can't you talk to me?" Lindsey pleaded angrily.

I looked at her. Probably really for the first time. That was her real problem - she talked too much. Lindsey could never do anything, feel anything, be anything. She had to tear apart and analyze first. Drown in a quagmire of thought, stagnate. Ruin everything by tainting it with subtle innuendo, hidden messages, and double meanings. What are you left with when you dissect and examine? Nothing but jagged pieces. I subscribed to the School of Situational Ethics. Never could be sure what I was going to do until post mortem.

"I'm gonna go," I replied, surprising even me.

Lindsey turned back to the TV. I knew she was going to start crying. It made me want to leave that much more.

"Uh... Goodbye." My feet knew their way out so they carried me across the living room and down the hall. I stopped to unlock the front door and there it was on top of this little antique table in the front hall. An 8x10" framed family portrait. Classic. Lindsey's father smiling goofily, her mother frowning, her little brother Kent looking cherubic and Lindsey staring pointedly into the camera, half a smile on her face. I couldn't help myself. I grabbed the picture and shut the front door.

This photo used to aggravate me to no end. Perfect fucking nuclear family. No mess, no hassle, no unsightly stains. I had walked maybe two blocks looking at the picture when I finally lost it. The anger welled up inside me like a fever. What was it about that picture that bugged me so much? Was it their ideal family unit or her parents' happy relationship that I was so jealous of? Or the fact that Lindsey had thrown me on the heap so easily, on Valentine's Day? Before I could decide, I punched out the glass and threw the ruined frame into the gutter under a parked car. The poetic justice was too much for me.

Oh well, I thought, Miller time. I made it back to #1 Super Markette, loaded up on two 40-ounce Mickey's and a Big Grab bag of Lay's Potato Chips and walked back to the Panhandle to see if I could catch up with those guys. No such luck. By the time I got there all that was left was a couple of crushed white cans and an empty twelve-pack box. Cops must have rousted them already. I miss all the fun.

All I could do was sit down on the cold, damp picnic bench, pull my Derby a little tighter around me and open the first 40. The Mickey's made me feel warmer and a little bit better. I sat there swilling my beer and thinking about everything and nothing all at once.

It was good to just watch the fog swirl overhead and drip out of the trees in staccato drops. My bony butt was cold where it came in contact with the park bench. Everything smelled wet and earthy. The streetlight down the block would disappear, come back and be swallowed up again by the fog. It was dark, cold and quiet. I liked it. One of the last things I remembered was cracking open the second 40 and heaving the empty at a garbage can a few yards away. My luck seemed to be improving because my shot was a perfect ringer. The bottle exploded with a satisfying smash as it hit bottom. The next time I talk to her is gonna be hell, I remembered thinking to myself.

I looked at the phone I was clutching in my hand. What would you do? I quickly hung up. Ah shit, so that's what happened, I half chuckled and half sobbed to myself.

I started along Van Ness again. Automatically, I made the turn and began walking up Fulton, thinking about Lindsey. Things weren't that bad, were they? Sure, she had been pissed off recently but wasn't she always? Running over what little I could remember of the last two weeks, I couldn't think of anything specific I'd done. It was a moot point anyway. She had just gotten sick of my drunken three ring circus. The joke had finally worn thin. It always does. Am I that pathetic, I asked myself. I didn't want to know the answer to that one.

I had forgotten all about The Mouth until I walked under the freeway overpass again. I was looking down at my falling feet again, trying to decide on a rhythm. My hips ached already. My head snapped up as the cold shadow fell upon me. I looked around wildly. The knot tightened in my stomach. I could feel my heart thumping in my chest as I stood rooted to the sidewalk. The wind whipped past me, tugging at my jacket, urging me to run. After a quick survey of the underpass turned up nothing but a bunch of pigeon shit out by the curb, I started back up Fulton feeling foolish.

Jesus Christ, what scared me so much about The Mouth? I laughed at myself. He's just some old vagrant. Must of migrated down to Market Street for the afternoon. Hang out with the rest of the feral humans.

A cop car cruised slowly by me as I floundered up Fulton. Johnny Law in the passenger seat eyed me suspiciously. Why do they always do that? I felt like I was guilty until proven innocent, a criminal. Tried to think of what I'd done, but aside from drinking in the Panhandle the night before and the time we kicked over all those newspaper machines, I couldn't figure it out. I guess neither could they because they sped off, leaving me to choke on their exhaust fumes.

Before I realized it, I was standing in front of #1 Super Markette. My feet had a mind all their own because they carried me on inside and into the back. They were out of Mickey's, I noticed as my eyes scanned the cold beer selection, so I grabbed a 40-ouncer of Miller and headed up towards the counter to pay.

"Hey, what's up, Sam?" I grunted.

Sam was behind the register, reading a *National Enquirer*, like he always did at this time, I guess. I wasn't sure because I was usually at work around then. He regarded me suspiciously.

"Aren't you supposed to be at work?" Sam barked at me. I was surprised. Something had changed.

"Uh... I got fired," I mumbled.

We looked at each other silently. Sam's attitude spelled it all out for me: indifference, annoyance, disgust.

"Two bucks," he said automatically, distantly. I abandoned the two dollar bills and walked home feeling stupid and ashamed.

We lived in the downstairs flat of a decaying two story Victorian. It had been painted off-white or cream colored once. That paint job had flaked off long before we moved in. The house now had the gray sun-bleached color of exposed wood.

The landlady lived in the flat above us. She was a wrinkled, stooped over little old lady who "hadn't been up to Divisadero in fifteen years." I never heard anything from that upstairs flat. No music, TV, or telephone. I used to lay awake at night wondering what the fuck was going on above my head. After imagining several gruesome scenarios involving transients, duct tape, and a cordless carving knife, I decided she was hiding from her death up there. Shut in, hoping to keep him shut out. Maybe she could wait her mortality out. Live forever behind a locked door.

I looked up the stairs at the front door. No use in trying to muster the strength to climb the stairs. No keys, remember? Now what the fuck was I going to do? The stench of wet, rotting garbage drifted over from underneath the stairs, making me want to gag viciously. That did it. I exploded. I walked down the driveway.

Next to the garage was a small locked door that led to the back porch by way of a dark, cramped hallway. When I got to that door I paused, then gave it a kick at the lock. I mean, I put everything I had into it, all my anger, just like a cop. Starsky and Hutch, eat your hearts out. The door jam gave way with a satisfying squeal and half of it fell inwards as the door bounced open. KRZ: 1, Doorjamb: 0. Wondered if I would be able to nail it back together as I slipped through the door and shut it the best I could behind me. I made it down the hall and into the backyard.

There was nowhere to sit but the top step of the back stairs, so I took that and looked over this dead little garden that took up most of the tiny backyard. A couple of shaggy shrubs squatted over by the back fence, in front of which the withered branches of three dead rose bushes poked up out of the ground. Weeds had taken over what was left of the little lawn surrounding a six foot wide oblong patch of exposed dirt. The flower bed next to the left fence was full of rocks, dirt clods and not much else. Pretty sad, not even a small tree. At some time the landlady must have taken care of her garden but that must have been a lifetime ago. Probably before she became obsessed with her death.

I tore off the top of the 40-ouncer and took a swig. It was cold and the carbonation in the first pull burned my throat. The familiar taste was comforting somehow. Another hit and I began thinking about the last time we had sex. I remembered it had been good.

It was one of those rare Sundays when Lindsey had the house to herself. Her parents and brother had gone to the flea market in Marin county. They made that pilgrimage across the Golden Gate Bridge occasionally. Lindsey's father was on a religious quest for the perfect antique. It could have been the battered rolltop desk in the basement he said he'd get around to refinishing or the stained glass window and frame hanging on the wall in Lindsey's room above her bed, but he wasn't sure. He was certain he'd know it when he saw it. Which tended to be every time they went to a yard sale, auction, or swap meet. Lindsey's mom and dad would inevitably come home arguing about some piece of dilapidated furniture or bric-a-brac he had or hadn't bought.

Lindsey begged off with the old "Gotta go to work" standby.

I walked up to the house just as they were taking off. Kent waved to me sadly from the rear window. Poor little bastard didn't want to go either. Hadn't perfected his excusatory skills yet. I gave him a nod of the head, hoping to inspire confidence. I don't think it worked.

Lindsey opened the door for me as I mounted the top stair. She stood just inside the doorway. Her long dark hair was combed to the side and over the shoulder. A strand hung in her mouth. She was in sweatpants, sweater and socks, no make-up. She looked beautiful. I stepped up close to her and leaned forward.

"Hi," I whispered.

"Hi," she replied and smiled.

I kissed her. Softly at first. She put her hand on the back of my neck and opened her mouth. Our tongues touched lightly, the first contact like an electrical spark. The minty flavor of toothpaste rode her breath but under that was the subtle taste of her saliva. My hands made their way around to the small of her back and pulled her closer to me. Lindsey smelled sweet, like she had just gotten out of the shower. I could feel myself start to get hard. She shivered so I let go.

"Get inside, girl," I teased her. "It's butt cold out here."

I followed Lindsey down the hall, past the living room and into the kitchen. She had obviously been cleaning up. Sunday morning's breakfast dishes lay drying in the dish rack. The window above the sink was fogged over with steam. Lindsey made a motion to wipe off the counter but I grabbed her around the waist before she could start. I kissed her hard, backing her up against the stove. She started to return my kisses. We stood there for a second lip-locked. I could feel the pressure of her crotch against mine.

"Not here," Lindsey said, breaking away. I looked at her sheepishly and hoped Lindsey wouldn't notice my erection. What was I thinking? She didn't have a microscope.

"Want anything to eat?" she motioned to the refrigerator to change the subject.

"Naw," I replied. "That's cool."

"What's the matter? Too hungover?" Lindsey snapped irritably. Funny how her mood changed like that. Like walking on tacks. I hated it. Made me want to fuck with her.

"Not really," I lied to smooth things over. "Grabbed something at the house."

"I'm going to finish up in here. Why don't you watch some TV?" she suggested.

Instead of going into the living room, I went up the stairs, turned left and into Lindsey's room. It was immaculate. A place for everything and everything in its place. Desktop clean. Neat pile of books, two pens side by side. I bet her underwear was folded and arranged neatly in its drawer but didn't have the guts to look.

It gave me the fucking creeps. I felt like I was soiling her room just by being there. Contaminating it with my festering presence.

I jumped on her bed diagonally, kicked off my shoes, turned on the little black and white on her nightstand and spun the dial. Kung-Fu Theater was on channel 26. My favorite. Cliché dialogue poorly dubbed over random lip movements.

It was easy to fall into the plot. Classic revenge motif with a 'boy meets girl, etc.' subplot done in rural Chinese. The villains were just beating the crap out of the hero's girl. I didn't hear Lindsey slip into the room. She crawled onto the bed.

"Whatya watchin'? Pay attention to me," Lindsey whined jokingly.

Man, they were working that bitch over. It took me a second to answer. "Kung-Fu Theater."

She sighed, annoyed, and fell back on the bed in a huff. I turned to look at her. I could tell she was irritated as I sat up.

"Hey you, pretty girl," I said in my best Chinese accent, the words totally out of sync with my mouth a la Kung-Fu Theater. "Come here."

Lindsey looked over at me, but obviously didn't get the joke. She was pouting.

"I said, 'Hey you, pretty girl.'" I tried again, "Come here."

Lindsey smiled but didn't move. I leaned forward and kissed her lightly. No resistance so I crawled forward and laid on top of her. Lindsey's knee came up, cupping my hips. She was kissing me hard back, breathing. I could feel her hand move lightly on my back, tracing a looping pattern. I let go of her mouth with mine and moved it down to her neck. She smelled like her hair conditioner. I bit her neck gently and my lips found their way up to the junction of throat and jaw, just below the ear.

"That tickles," she giggled, pulling her head back.

Our mouths came together again and I could feel both her hands on my back. I was leaning on my left arm, I could feel it going numb. My right hand went up her sweater. I managed to undo the frontal snapping bra with one hand. Damn, I was getting better at this.

Lindsey's nipples were erect. Her breast felt good in my hand.

I pulled her sweater up around her shoulders and brought my mouth down to her nipple. Pale skin, her breasts a shade lighter, no tan line. I could barely trace the outline of a blue vein on the underside of one breast. They were round and firm, with small sized nipples set high.

Lindsey sat up and tugged off the sweater, slipping her bra off. I got out of my Pendleton and pulled off the t-shirt underneath. We lay back, naked from the waist up. It was cold but her body was warm, and I swear I could feel static electricity generated by our skin rubbing together while we kissed.

There were goosebumps on both our bodies. I licked Lindsey's belly button and began untying her sweats. She lifted her ass up as they came free and I pulled them off. God, she was beautiful. Dark hair, creamy skin, slim body, no gut to speak of. I sat up, unbuttoned my jeans and got down to my boxers. Lindsey pulled me back down and attacked my mouth with hers.

I put my hand on her white panties. I could feel the heat and wetness through the material. She caught her breath as I pulled them to one side and ran a finger up her slit. The floodgates were open. I found her clitoris with my finger. It was hard so I wormed my way down between her legs, tore off her panties and threw them on the rug. She spread her legs.

Her open vagina stared me in the face. I noticed that even though she kept her pubic hair shorter than mine she had a bigger patch. She smelled slightly musty but not unpleasant. It turned me on. I pulled the lips open and licked her twice with the flat of my tongue like a cat. She tasted kind of salty. I found her clitoris, encircled it with my mouth and rolled it between my lips. Lindsey sighed and ran her fingers through my hair. I looked up. She closed her eyes and arched her back. I could barely see her face. What was she thinking about?

"Do you like that?" I asked in a husky voice.

"Uh huh," she mumbled.

I reached up with one hand, pinched a nipple, made my tongue stiff and went back down on her. I was using my whole face. My legs hung halfway off the bed, painfully right at the knees. My throbbing erection dug into the sheet and my neck began to ache from the constant up and down, side to side motion. I heard Lindsey gasp and her grip tightened on my hair. Her clitoris had changed to a deep red, verging on purple. I increased my tempo. Lindsey's body shook. I could feel her orgasm underneath me. She cried out then relaxed.

I climbed up and wiped my mouth off on the sheet. Fuck, I was sweating already. A hair was plastered to the back of my throat and I gagged trying to scrape it off with my tongue. Finally it came free and I spit it out. Lindsey pulled my head down and our lips locked again.

"Put it on," she said breathily.

I knew what she meant so I sat up and began going through my pants.

"Goddamit, it has to be here somewhere." I found the condom in my front pocket, yanked off my boxers and tore it open. I sat on the edge of the bed and tried to put it on. This was my biggest nightmare. I had this reoccurring vision of Lindsey's mother walking in as I was hunched over trying to slip latex over my little swollen penis. A fate worse than death. I got the condom on with little embarrassment and less hassle. Lindsey reached up and guided me in as I lay down on top of her. I reached down and pulled her knees up.

"Wait a minute," I said, laying perfectly still. I could feel myself inside of her. She was hot and wet. It was excruciating. I began with a few slow pumps. Lindsey threw her head back and to one side. Her dark hair was splayed out on the pillow underneath her like a fan. I could smell the sweet scent of her body as I raised myself up on my arms and quickened my pace. I was building towards orgasm but the condom held me back. A thought crossed my mind: we were two cats, fucking or fighting as if our lives depended on it.

Rip her in half, fuck her to death. I was John Holmes, Ted Bundy, and James Dean all wrapped up into one goddamn sick machine. We had fallen into a vicious rhythm. She answered every thrust with one of her own like a mirror image. Lindsey was so tight, I could feel every ring of muscle gripping my erect dick. I was in heaven, I couldn't take anymore. My orgasm snuck up on me like a freight train. I dug in my toes and groaned as I let go. My heartbeat thundered in my ears. God, it felt good.

I slumped forward and laughed. I couldn't help it. I knew what kind of stupid faces I made at that magic moment. Lindsey didn't say anything. I sat up and pulled the condom off with a wet snap. Now that hurt.

What the fuck was I going to do with it? I tossed it on the floor for future reference, throw it away later on. I lay down next to Lindsey spoon fashion and kissed the back of her neck. We were both naked and sweaty. The room smelled like burning sex. I lay there for a couple of minutes not saying anything, dozing off.

"Shit, I'm gonna be late!" Lindsey screamed, looking at her clock and snapping me out of my daze.

"Just a couple of minutes more," I murmured. "You've still got fifteen minutes."

"Not if I want to be on time," she replied, jumping up. For her, being on time meant showing up five minutes early. This was annoyingly pointless if you asked me. Just meant they got five free minutes out of you. Lindsey was dressed and brushing her hair in record time. I was still naked.

"Look, I gotta go. Lock the door as you leave," she said, slipping out of the bedroom. "Bye."

I heard her walk down the stairs and out the front door with a slam. I lay there for a couple of minutes not quite knowing what to do. I figured I should get dressed and cut out before her parents came home. I had my boxers on and was looking for my t-shirt when the phone rang. I debated answering it and decided against it until the seventh ring.

"Hello," I said awkwardly.

"Hello, is Lindsey home?" asked a sultry female voice.

"No, she's not. Can I take a message?"

"Yes, this is Andrea, from her work. I was wondering if Lindsey could come in for me next Friday night," she purred.

"Hold on a second...," I mumbled, looking for a pen. "Andrea...," I sighed, kneeling down next to Lindsey's nightstand to scribble the message.

"Oh, I liked that," she cooed seductively, "say that again."

"Huh!?" I didn't know what to say. Damn, I had no idea who this girl was but that kind of did something for me. I was gonna have to check her out. Drop by all unexpected like down at the restaurant.

"What's happenin' Friday?" I finally managed to blurt out.

"This new club, Club 2F8, is opening on Fourth and Brannan, where Don't Kick The Dog used to be. You should check it out."

"Maybe I will," I said, hanging up the phone and writing down her message. I finally found most of my clothes and let myself out of the front door. Never did find that damn t-shirt.

I had finished about two-thirds of my 40-ouncer while I replayed this tired memory in my mind. The bottle was going warm in my hand. I leaned back against the weathered doorjamb of the back door. The top step felt hard underneath my bony butt but not unpleasant. I could feel the grain of the wood through my thin work pants. I stared out at the sad little garden as I downed the last swallows of High Life. A robin glided down out of the lead-colored sky and landed on the walk at the foot of the steps.

He was beautiful: red breast, brown wings, strutting walk, the cocky way he stared at me out of the side of his head. His eyes were shiny black marbles, huge for such a small skull. I realized it was the first robin I had seen in a few months. It surprised me because I didn't usually notice those kind of things. I sat as motionless as I could, watching my newfound friend. I wanted to speak to him but didn't know what to say.

"I'd offer you a sip of my beer," I whispered, "but I'm all out."

The robin cocked his head to the side, searching for the origin of this disturbance. He took a couple of arrogant steps, sizing me up. I guessed the robin decided I was harmless because he soon lost interest in me. He surveyed the confines of the little garden slowly. Nothing caught his eye. A couple of short hops took the robin to the middle of the lawn/dirt patch. Must have realized there was nothing for him there because he took off like a shot.

I know how you feel, I thought to myself, a little bit lonely, staring up at the empty sky. I leaned my head back and shut my eyes trying to soak up what little warmth I could. I was asleep before I knew it. The blackness came on mercilessly.

The sound of the Old Lady slamming her car door in the driveway snapped me awake. I couldn't have been asleep more than two hours. My back ached dully from being cramped in one position for so long.

On Fridays my mother would work through her half-hour lunch break, eating at her desk, so she could leave early. Come 4:30 she was gone Johnson. I heard her fumble with her keys and open the front door. She didn't notice the busted side door.

"I guess it's time to go for a walk." I slipped out of the splintered doorway, tucked my empty 40-ouncer in one of the garbage cans and headed up the block. Shit, I couldn't think of anywhere to go. I just stood vacantly on the corner, trying to decide on a destination. Only four directions available but somehow I got the feeling I was headed straight down. One of those giddy, light-headed, here-you-go, bottom drops out of your world type of feelings.

Oh well, I figured, a trip around the block is good enough. Man, it was weird, I guessed I had been working too much because I barely recognized the neighborhood in the darkening twilight. I used to be a local but now everything seemed unfamiliar, distorted, threatening. I was captivated by the shadows. I never noticed how many deep pockets of blackness lurked in the neighborhood. Doorways, alleys, and garages submerged in pools of inky darkness.

Shit, there I was in front of the house again. The lights were on in the living room. My breath was a plume of steam in the cold night air. I could feel the snot begin running out of my nose. Now what? I ran up the stairs and rang the doorbell. I could hear the Old Lady walk down the hall calling out, "Hold on a second," as she came.

She unbolted the locks on the front door but left on the chain and opened it a crack. The aroma of a baking TV dinner rode out on the escaping cushion of warm air, causing my stomach to grumble.

"What are you doing home so early?" she asked in an accusatory tone. They always expected the worst. I noticed she hadn't opened the door any wider.

"Look," I answered in a weary voice, "let me in."

Moms undid the chain and stepped out of my way as I pushed my way in.

"What are you doing home so early?" The Old Lady repeated to my back as it made its way down the hall towards my room. I turned around halfway down the dark hallway. What would you tell her?

"They let me off early. Things were slow, there wasn't much to do." This at least sounded good. I mean, it was partially true. ALF had never let me off early before but he did this time. Permanently. Best rationalization I could think of at the moment, but given a second I'm sure I could come up with something a whole lot better.

I made it back to my cluttered room and flopped on the bed. Lay there for a couple of minutes face down in my pillow. It began to smother me but that was alright. There were times when I thought quietly to myself, "Maybe I want to die."

I mean, sure, I thought about killing myself sometimes but could never decide on a good way to do it. I tried them on for size but never felt comfortable with the results. Sleeping pill OD, blow my brains out, Golden Gate dive: they all sounded too iffy. Like I'd miss, or fuck up and become a catatonic vegetable until the insurance money ran out then be parted out as an organ donor for people who had the cash. Let's face it, there are no good ways to die, just messy, horrible ones and anybody who tells you different is a fool. I wanted to live. However, death did have its advantages.

I wasn't going out like that no matter what my brain wanted. My lungs began to burn and my body spasmed, demanding oxygen.

I jerked my head up and gasped for breath. The blood rushed in my ears. I saw spots. The air tasted better than I remembered. I rolled over on my back. Noticed I had an erection. Hated to die without one of those.

I looked around, gulping for air. It felt strange being in my room. Like being in someone else's bedroom uninvited. Alien, almost as if I didn't belong. Too quiet beside the thud of my heart.

Maybe it will help if I take off my jacket. It didn't. I just lay there on my back, gritting my teeth, scanning the still room. I couldn't take it, something had to break.

Finally I stood up, yanked off the bow tie and threw it into the trashcan across the room. That made me feel better, so the white shirt and apron followed suit. Hell, I could always use the black pants.

I laid back down, goose bumps and all, on the bed in my boxers and looked over at the nightstand. The digital alarm clock read 5:18. It was dark already outside. My vato Miles would be getting off work at 6:00 sharp. He worked at the Levitz Furniture Showroom in South San Francisco. Started in Carpets but had recently made the big career move to Assistant Manager of Oriental Rugs. They were grooming him for bigger things.

"Talk about making it," these were his own words, "Oriental Rugs are my life."

He could tell the difference between machine and handmade rugs at twenty paces. Even worse, he liked to talk about it. It was almost to the point where I could tell you the benefits and drawbacks of different fiber and dye combinations, and I didn't even give a fuck. I mean, couldn't he give it a rest?

I had known Miles since the first day of high school. We were in the same homeroom together, and initially I didn't like him. Everything came too easy for him. He always knew what to say and when to say it, while I stayed silent and sat in the back of the room.

I guess I was jealous. People took an instant liking to Miles. He was voted homeroom rep the first week and sat in a desk in front of me. I hated looking at the back of his head. Sometimes

Miles would have a zit on the back of his neck, right below the hairline. A huge whitehead. It never failed to gross me out. Made me want to reach out and smack him one in the back of his head. Turned out Miles lived a couple of blocks away from the Old Lady, so we ended up riding the bus together. Been hanging around with him off and on ever since. Might as well go see what he's up to, I thought. Don't have anything better to do.

Tell him about getting fired. Miles would probably get a good laugh out of it. Hopefully, I could borrow the Old Lady's Ford Maverick. She wasn't using it anyway. Never did anything with her Friday nights except watch the idiot box, drink a couple of glasses of cheap white wine and fall asleep on the couch. It wasn't like she was an alcoholic or anything, just liked her white wine.

I got up from the bed and walked over to the pile of dirty clothes spilling out of my open closet. Picked through the heap and pulled on some jeans, my Nikes, a semi-clean t-shirt, and a black sweatshirt. My wallet, keys, and some spare change were on the dresser where I dropped them the night before. The Derby made the outfit complete.

I slipped out of the room and made my way down the hall. The Old Lady was in the living room watching TV, drinking a glass of white wine and eating her microwave bounty. It was a Weight Watchers Seafood Linguini TV Dinner, I noticed. The Old Lady followed the Weight Watchers regime religiously.

I guessed that way she could be sure I wouldn't touch her food because there was no way in hell you could get me to eat that crap. It used to piss me off to no end. If, on the off chance, I should happen to come home hungry (heaven forbid) the only thing to eat in the house was food-lite. Shit will kill you. Turn to some as of yet undetected carcinogen in your intestine. The Old Lady looked up from a forkful.

"Hey, Moms, I was gonna pick Miles up from work. Do you think I could borrow your car for a couple of hours?"

She took a bite and thought about it. She liked Miles. Last time Miles had been over he had complimented her Pakistani Bokhara.

Talking about the rug in the living room. It was an old hand-me-down from my grandmother. "Cut the Eddie Haskell shit," I told him later on.

"I guess so," she said suspiciously, eyes narrowing. "The keys are in my purse."

I got them. "Thanks, Moms," I said over my shoulder as I jetted out the front door.

"Be careful," she screamed, not looking up from the TV as the door slammed.

That rusty old piece of shit was parked in the driveway. I thought about getting some more beer as I slipped behind the wheel but just couldn't bring myself to go back into #1 Super Markette. That sort of humiliation I definitely didn't need. I drove across Divisadero and down 17th through the Mission on my way to 101 south.

It felt good to put some distance behind me. I fantasized about just driving off and never coming back, but couldn't figure out where to go. I stopped at this little Mom & Pop liquor store near Army Street and copped a six-pack of Mickey's, no problem. Just walked right in and helped myself like it was the most natural thing in the world. They overcharged me $1.90, no questions asked.

Fuck Sam. I can still score elsewhere, I was thinking as I pulled into the Levitz Furniture Showroom parking lot.

I threw it in park in a spot where I could see through the front doors, but back out of the way so I wasn't obvious. My watch read 6:06 p.m. but I had set it three minutes fast so as not to be too late to work. It didn't work. Miles would be out at any second.

I could see the night manager closing out the front registers through the doors. He was counting money and talking to someone just out of sight. I opened the first Mickey's and put the Big Mouth up to mine. That initial cold gulp twisted my mind out of its funk. I could imagine Mr. Night Manager giving out some cryptic advice on how to claw your way to the top of the Levitz Furniture corporate ladder. 'Pay for Performance' or some equally inane cliché. He just kept counting and talking. I kept on drinking.

It was 6:14. I had just finished my first Mickey's, crammed it back into the six-pack and tore open a second. Finally the other half of the Levitz Furniture corporate ladder climbing seminar moved into view. I choked in mid-swallow. It was Miles. He was doing a little post-shift shmoozing. Mr. Night Manager held Miles' rapt attention. He was hunched over, listening subserviently. God, it made me sick. I drained my second Mickey's and opened a third. That kind of self-important, pompous asshole was everywhere, like a cancer. They sucked the life right out of you with their snide comments and tunnel vision. Leave you all dry and hollow inside like them.

Finally he was done closing up the registers, which was good. I didn't know if I could take much more. Mr. Night Manager gathered up that evening's receipts, unlocked the doors and let Miles out. He stood there for a second, unsure of exactly what to do, while Mr. Night Manager locked him out. Puzzled, Miles looked over at the Maverick, one of the only cars in the lot, which I happened to be in. I rolled down the window and heaved an empty as far as I could at him across the parking lot. It shattered with a lonely pop, not even two-thirds of the distance between us. Couldn't be anyone else but me. Miles dashed over and tore open the passenger door.

"What the fuck do you think you're doing?" he asked angrily, between clenched teeth. "I work here."

"Just trying to put the fear of God into you," I replied glibly.

Miles had no answer for that so he slid into the passenger seat and shut the door.

"Relax, no one's around," I offered, handing him the six-pack. "Want a beer?"

He took one and unscrewed the cap. I started the car and pulled out of the parking lot. We were rolling up 101 north, not saying anything. I was concentrating on the shifting patterns of traffic, Big Mouth between my legs. I took a couple of hits off it when there was a lull in the action. Miles must have been obsessed with getting to the bottom of his beer because he stared down into the bottle quietly. There were a couple of moments of strained silence. He took a long suck off of his Mickey's.

"I talked to Lindsey today," Miles finally admitted.

I yanked my eyes away from the silent freeway and looked over at him. What the fuck was that supposed to mean? If he was wondering what was up with me, why didn't he come right out and say so? Hinting around only made my jaws clamp shut tighter.

To tell the truth, I didn't know what I felt. Rage, sorrow, regret. The conflicting emotions swirled into a gray mass I sat there wrestling with. Just when I thought I could put a name to my emotions, they'd downshift in a crazy manic mood swing. I didn't want to hastily blurt out something I didn't feel.

That was just it. I wanted to be absolutely sure of my emotions before I could express them for fear of inadvertently hurting someone I cared for. I didn't want to be like my Old Man, but that's what was paralyzing me.

"Say what you mean and mean what you say," my father told me, even if he couldn't live up to it himself.

A familiar feeling crept over me. The gnawing guilt feeling. Guilt over fucking up again, but I was doomed from the start. It was inevitable. Collision course from the word 'Go'. I was almost resigned to it. Never could live up to someone else's expectations, let alone my own.

There's always that final straw and you know what happens to the camel's back. Other than that, anything else was pointless. It was a done deal. It seemed anticlimactic, almost cliché. No fireworks, she just gave up. I automatically made the transition to 101 north where it splits with 80 east across the Bay Bridge.

Am I that jaded, I asked myself. I guessed I needed extremes to make me feel anything. I should have just dowsed myself with unleaded and struck the match. Go out screaming, kicking, burning. Those last few seconds before the spark caught would be everything.

"How's she doin'?" I finally asked, rolling down the Fell Street exit.

Miles must have realized I didn't want to talk about it because he had gone back to staring into his beer. Now I was annoyed. None of his fucking business what I felt. It was better not to think about it. Like scratching at a scab, it only leaves a bigger scar.

"Dude, I gotta take back the Old Lady's car," I informed Miles as we pulled up on his parents' home.

"Hey, man, thanks for the ride," he replied, eyeing his front door nervously.

Finally cut loose the dead weight, I thought as I patched out the best that old piece of shit could, in front of Miles' parents' house. His folks had probably already peeped out of their curtains like the timid pocket mice they were. Fuck 'em. Rattle their cage.

I pulled into the driveway of the house, barely. Some yuppie asshole had parked his Volvo stationwagon hanging halfway into our driveway. I should have just tossed a brick through the front windshield and found a spot down the block. That might teach him a little courtesy.

I got out of the car, locked the door, and hustled up the block. The wind was whipping down the street against me as I turned the corner. It was fucking cold. I had my hands buried deep in my pockets and was half running as I turned into #1 Super Markette. Just my luck, someone was coming out at the same time.

He was drinking one of those cheap artificially-flavored fruit punch drinks that comes in 10-ounce plastic bottles. Our impact caused his lower lip to lose its grip on the rim of the bottle and red sugar water to leap out onto his white turtleneck sweater. I looked up at the victim.

Dark flat top, short on the sides, no sideburns whatsoever, and long, long in the back. A thin gold chain hung around the white turtleneck. Stocky for 5'8". Could have been Mexican, Filipino, or Caucasian. It was hard to tell. Just looked like a typical seventeen-year-old WPOD. It wasn't so much ethnic origin but more of an attitude, a way of holding your face. Belligerent machismo. Thin mustache made the outfit complete. Complete asshole. His three identically uniformed companions busted up as he stared down at the Rorshach ink blot on his chest in red. I wonder what he saw?

The WPOD's head jerked up.

"Sorry about that, man," I muttered, as I shouldered my way past his friends.

The WPOD gave me a dirty look as his buddies had a good laugh at his expense. I walked to the back and helped myself to a 40-ouncer from the dairy case. That was totally fucked up but it was an accident. I mean sure, it was kind of funny but I didn't mean to bump into him. I felt bad for staining his turtleneck.

Oh well, fuck him. Time to pay up. I placed my 40 on the counter. Sam put his hand on it. There was a pause.

"What was wrong with those guys?" I asked Sam to break the silence.

"They tried to purchase beer without a license," he replied. Sounded ominous. We looked at each other for a few seconds more. "$1.98," he said once again in that distant, annoyed voice.

This obviously isn't going to work too many more times. I surrendered the bills meekly. Sam tucked the bottle into a brown paper bag. I said my one-sided goodbye and walked out about one inch tall. I guess I'm just another loser in Sam's eyes, I couldn't help but think to myself.

I felt like a worthless piece of shit as I began to walk down the block towards the house. There's gotta be something better than this, I thought as I passed a particularly dark driveway.

I didn't see the punch coming out of the blackness but it caught me right behind the left ear. Perfect cold-cock sucker-shot, unexpected and vicious. I saw a flash of light behind my eyes and heard my 40-ouncer smash as it hit pavement. My momentum carried me forwards and down to my knees. Seemed like it took minutes, not seconds. There was a ringing in my ears like a TV test pattern

"Sorry about that, man," spat a voice full of venom.

It was the WPOD I had spilled the fruit punch on. I could see the hulking shapes of his three friends behind him. They were giggling like little girls. Four on one, perfect WPOD odds. I tried to get up to run. The second punch, a good right uppercut, went straight to my left eye. More stars, like an explosion in my head.

Back down to the concrete. I tried to get up again. The WPOD took two steps forward and caught me hard in the stomach with his foot, his face a snarling mask of pure hatred. My breath exploded out of me and I felt the knot in my stomach burst like a wet paper bag. My mouth went sticky and I could taste the metallic flavor of blood.

I coughed and gagged at the same time, fighting for air. I had to get up or I was dust. I tried to look up. The WPOD moved in for the kill. The next kick caught me squarely in the head as I was down on all fours retching. My head swiveled back on its neck and I slumped forward. Another kick racked my frame.

"Jesus Christ, you're gonna kill him," was the last thing I heard.

The darkness swallowed me up. I could feel my consciousness being stripped away as I fell into its pit. I was drowning in a sea of nothing, seeing nothing and feeling nothing. It was comforting and suffocating, like coming home to the womb. Finally, even my point of reference evaporated. I wasn't ready for what happened next.

I was in my room at my parents' old house, laying on my back, looking at the closed bedroom door. My little bathrobe hung on a hook on the back of the door. I was tiny compared to the huge single bed. It felt weird to be six again, even the nightstand looked monstrous. My little hands were clenched in chubby fists. Something horrible was about to happen. I was about to die. I knew it instinctually. Right there, lying in my oversized bed.

A knot of terror had formed deep in my throat, causing my breath to come in ragged gasps. Fight or flight syndrome, adrenaline OD. My heart was racing, pulse thundering in my ears. I had this insane urge to get up and run, but I lay there transfixed by the whole familiar scene. The bedroom door was pushed open and there he stood just inside the doorway, framed by the rectangle of light coming through my open door.

His face was hidden in the shadows by the glare coming from the hall, but I could tell it was my father. He just stood there staring at me. I stared back, horrified. We looked at each other for what seemed an eternity. It started to bug me. What the fuck was he looking at? I was sick of people staring at me, making their little judgments. The rage grew inside me like a flame. My tiny eight-year-old body began to shake with anger. He took a step into my room.

My father was dressed in his favorite Pendleton shirt and neon green lycra bike shorts. Two gold chains nestled in his thick black chest hair. Greasy brown hair was parted perfectly down the middle, exposing pearl-studded ears. I was trapped by his intently staring eyes like a rat hypnotized by a hungry snake.

His eyes narrowed as his mouth split into a grin. The lips kept pulling back further and further, until I was sure his head would split. His lips were pulled taut over yellowed teeth and bleeding gums. The gums had receded, grown so far back that his teeth resembled huge stained and pitted ivory tusks. Decay had engraved its twisted path across the ruined enamel like illegible hieroglyphics. I couldn't believe the size of those teeth. How the fuck did they all fit inside of that mouth? Like some godforsaken human piranha cannibal. I stared into the mouth fascinated. A film of crust had filled the gap between canine and eye tooth and a fleck of spit was caught way up in a corner of that huge mouth.

"I been watchin' you, boy," hissed the mouth.

That did it. "That's all I can stands and I can't stands no more." I fucking snapped. I was so sick of this shit. I tore the covers off and yanked my ten-year-old prepubescent body out of bed to finally confront this motherfucker. This had been going on for too long. Better to die on your feet.

I began to walk across the room. I wanted to look my father in the eye. It was like walking underwater, every step took an eternity. Slowly my perspective changed. I gained a year with each step. Eleven, twelve, thirteen. The years mounted with every pissed off footfall. Finally, across the room, I stood nineteen years old and face to face with that bastard. I wrenched open my mute lips to say something, anything.

"Fuck you. Who are you to judge me?" I asked.

The whole scene freeze-framed. My father was trapped with a surprised look, wiping that smug grin off of his fucking face. The edges cracked and the whole thing fell in on itself like a broken mirror, leaving only the comforting darkness.

I can hear those small shore waves again, but as I concentrate on them they disintegrate and become the sound of my own ragged breathing. It comes in painful gasps. Something is torn deep in my burning side. A cough wracks my aching body, bringing more blood up into my mouth with a wet gurgle.

Another particularly large wave crashes somewhere above my head, pulling me up out of the hole. I try to open my eyes but one of them is swollen shut. A spot on my forehead burns from the scrape where it connected with cement. Through my ruined right eye I can make out the tail lights of the passing Fulton bus as it goes by, its sooty exhaust blowing in my face.

I'm laying face down on the sidewalk, my nose about six inches from the gutter. It's an odd perspective. The parked cars loom huge over me, threatening. My left arm is twisted painfully underneath me. My gut is tender but feels better, the knot in my stomach is gone. In its place is a calm empty feeling.

I pull myself up on all fours and spit a bloody wad into the gutter. I'm shaking uncontrollably, my teeth chattering.

Fuck all of you. You thought by judging me, laughing at me, turning your backs, you could put me in my place. Each day, try to strip more and more of my humanity. Beat me down, make me nothing, like you. Unfeeling, predictable, egocentric, dead.

And the worst part was, I actually cared. Worried what you thought of me, as if it mattered. Don't you realize by making me nothing in your eyes, all you did was let me loose, off the hook, free? There's a profound beauty in the number zero, the only real whole number, naked, hollow, complete. I will live my own life. It's what I need. I'm grateful for this opportunity. Every day teaches me something new.

I put the back of my hand up to my nose and it comes away

bloody. Not enough for another broken nose but that first kick sure cleaned my clock. My head throbs and the world swims alarmingly as I yank myself to my feet but I feel beautiful. I'm more alive now than ever. Every thought is crystalline, poignant in its urgency. Elation.

I now know what I have to do. I've got to make it home. It's about time I cut the umbilical chord.

Manic D Press
Books

Forty-Ouncer. *Kurt Zapata.* $9.95

The Hashish Man & other stories. *Lord Dunsany.* $9.95

Next Stop: Troubletown. *Lloyd Dangle.* $10.95

The Unsinkable Bambi Lake. *Bambi Lake with Alvin Orloff.* $11.95

Hell Soup. *Sparrow 13 LaughingWand.* $8.95

Revival: spoken word from Lollapalooza 94. *Edited by Juliette Torrez,*
    Liz Belile, Mud Baron & Jennifer Joseph. $12.95

The Ghastly Ones & Other Fiendish Frolics. *Richard Sala.* $9.95

The Underground Guide to San Francisco. *Jennifer Joseph, editor.* $10.95

King of the Roadkills. *Bucky Sinister.* $9.95

Alibi School. *Jeffrey McDaniel.* $8.95

Signs of Life: channel-surfing through '90s culture.
    Edited by Jennifer Joseph & Lisa Taplin. $12.95

Beyond Definition: new writing from gay & lesbian san francisco.
    Edited by Marci Blackman & Trebor Healey. $10.95

Love Like Rage. *Wendy-o Matik* $7.00

The Language of Birds. *Kimi Sugioka* $7.00

The Rise and Fall of Third Leg. *Jon Longhi* $9.95

Specimen Tank. *Buzz Callaway* $10.95

The Verdict Is In. *Edited by Kathi Georges & Jennifer Joseph* $9.95

Elegy for the Old Stud. *David West* $7.00

The Back of a Spoon. *Jack Hirschman* $7.00

Mobius Stripper. *Bana Witt* $8.95

Baroque Outhouse/The Decapitated Head of a Dog. *Randolph Nae* $7.00

Graveyard Golf and other stories. *Vampyre Mike Kassel* $7.95

Bricks and Anchors. *Jon Longhi* $8.00

The Devil Won't Let Me In. *Alice Olds-Ellingson* $7.95

Greatest Hits. *Edited by Jennifer Joseph* $7.00

Lizards Again. *David Jewell* $7.00

The Future Isn't What It Used To Be. *Jennifer Joseph* $7.00

Acts of Submission. *Joie Cook* $4.00

Zucchini and other stories. *Jon Longhi* $3.00

Standing In Line. *Jerry D. Miley* $3.00

Drugs. *Jennifer Joseph* $3.00

Bums Eat Shit and other poems. *Sparrow 13* $3.00

Into The Outer World. *David Jewell* $3.00

Solitary Traveler. *Michele C.* $3.00

Night Is Colder Than Autumn. *Jerry D. Miley* $3.00

Seven Dollar Shoes. *Sparrow 13 LaughingWand.* $3.00

Intertwine. *Jennifer Joseph.* $3.00

Now Hear This. *Lisa Radon.* $3.00

Bodies of Work. *Nancy Depper* $3.00

Corazon Del Barrio. *Jorge Argueta.* $4.00

Please add $2.00 to all orders
for postage and handling.

Send $1 for complete catalog.

Manic D Press

Box 410804

San Francisco CA 94141 USA

manicd@sirius.com
http://www.well.com/user/manicd/

distributed to the trade
in the US & Canada by
Publishers Group West

in the UK & Europe by
Turnaround Distribution